Dancing in Combat Boots

Also by Teresa R. Funke

Remember Wake

For Younger Readers

The Home-Front Heroes WWII Series
Doing My Part
The No-No Boys
V for Victory

Visit www.teresafunke.com to:

• Add your stories or your family's stories about WWII.

• Learn more about women's and children's experiences in World War II.

• Download a book club guide to *Dancing in Combat Boots* and to learn how to schedule Teresa to speak to your group.

Dancing in
Combat Boots

and Other Stories of
American Women in World War II

Teresa R. Funke

VICTORY
HOUSE
PRESS

Some of the stories in this collection were previously published in the following publications: "Las Estrellas de Oro" in *U.S. Catholic*, reprinted in *The Copperfield Review*; "Where She Began" in *High Plains Register*; "Three Thousand Men" in *The MacGuffin*; "Freer than I've Ever Been" in *Calyx*; "Living on the Wind" in *Kalliope*

This is a work of fiction. Names, places and some incidents have been changed.

Published by:
Victory House Press
3836 Tradition Drive
Fort Collins, Colorado 80526
www.victoryhousepress.com

Library of Congress Control Number: 2009936548

Printed in Canada

ISBN 978-1-935571-09-4
(Previously published by Bailiwick Press, ISBN 978-1-934649-00-8)

Acknowledgments

This book would simply not exist were it not for the many wonderful women who shared their World War II experiences with me. In addition to those whose stories appear in this book, I'd like to thank several others who offered me insights into that fascinating time period (several of whom have now passed away): Roslyn Arnstein, Shirley Brand, Edythe Brueck, Kate Carr, Jo Foxworth, Vera Long, Ginnie McCutcheon, Mary Settle, Kate Shearer, Evelyn Veillette, and Audrey Haakonstad, who started it all.

I'd also like to thank the female members of the Survivors of Wake, Guam and Cavite for welcoming me into their circle and sharing their memories with me.

It was interesting, in writing a book about women, to note how often my thoughts turned to the influential women who shepherded me into my own adult roles: my aunts Rose Marie Meierotto, Luz Beard, Celia Weston and Marlene Clouser; my stepmother Sally Rupp; my mother-in-law Mary Funke; and my friends Maria Andrijeski, Nancy Tacke, Lisa Lavin, Deanna Foerster, Ann Suarez and Lynne Funke; and, of course, my late grandmothers Celia Talamantez and Margaret Rupp.

Authors work in solitude, but never alone. I'd like to thank the following wonderful writers: Susan M. Stacy for guiding my interest in retelling true stories; Lisa Spires for picking me up when I was down; Susan Skog for spurring me ever onward; and especially my friends and fellow members of the Slow Sand Writers Society, who critiqued this book in all its incarnations and never stopped believing in its value. They are: Julia Doggart, Tracy Ekstrand, Kathy Hayes, Luana Heikes, Paul Miller, Leslie Patterson, Laura Pritchett, Jennifer Nastu, Laura Resau, Todd Shimoda, Greta Skau, Zach Zorich, and especially Jean Hanson.

Special thanks to Karla Oceanak, my writing and publishing partner. More than anyone else, she has seen promise in this book, and her careful reading, astute editing and constant reassurance helped make it what it is.

I'd also like to extend appreciation to Kendra Spanjer for bringing these women to life in such a wonderful cover illustration and Launie Parry for her superb cover design.

An author's journey begins at home. I'd like to thank my mother, Mary Helen Talamantez, for first championing my writing; my father, Larry Rupp, for helping me develop an appreciation for good literature; my brother, Mike Rupp, for challenging me with new ideas; my children, Brian, Lydia and Ava, for believing their mom is the best writer in the world; and my husband, Roger, whose love, encouragement and support make everything possible.

*For my mother, who modeled for me
all the roles women can play*

Contents

Author's Note

As a child, I longed for a grandfather to tell me stories of World War II. Perhaps because both of my grandfathers died before I knew them, I clung to that romanticized image of a child engrossed in an old man's tales. I must have wanted them to be larger than life—and nothing looms larger in our collective conscience than the war hero. Men and war; they are inextricably linked.

But what about the women who kept our nation running while the boys were away? They are mere footnotes in most of the dozens of books published about World War II each year. It's no wonder that it never occurred to me as a child to ask my grandmothers about their war stories. By the time a high school assignment set me wondering about women's roles in World War II, I'd lost my father's mother. My mother's mother was a no-nonsense introvert who could see little use in discussing the past. She told me only that she'd moved with a sister from San Antonio to Detroit to work in a war factory. I've often wondered what more I could have learned if I'd been more persistent, if I hadn't accepted her insistence that her contributions had been minimal, even trivial.

In 1990, while working as a research assistant for a PBS series, I was sent to interview an older gentleman about his role in the Battle of Wake Island and his subsequent capture by the Japanese. His stories of terror, brutality, injustice, camaraderie and courage afforded me that chance to listen to a real war hero. But I couldn't help noticing his wife, too—the vivacious woman who sat beside him and reminded him of details he was leaving out, who showed me newspaper clippings and scrapbooks she'd assembled, who invited me to a meeting of the POW survivors' organization to which she and her husband belonged. She'd taken his stories on as her own. His experience was her link to that time period, as it has become for so many wives of veterans.

Later, when I contacted her to tell me her war story, she was surprised to be asked (as were many of the women in this book). I found myself as engaged by her accounts as I had been by her husband's. Maybe it was partly the way she told her stories, the words and phrases she used to describe the "ordinary" life she'd led—a life of rationing, blackouts, war bond drives, national leaders as heroes, brothers turned soldiers, women entering the workforce, a nation galvanized behind a single cause. During that interview, she and I both realized she had more to offer than either of us expected, and I found myself wanting to hear more from the women of her generation.

The stories you are about to read are fiction, though each is closely based on the experiences of an actual woman. In most cases, only names and minor details have been changed. For this book, I sought out and interviewed women from across the country whose wartime contributions were typical in some ways, exceptional in others. I also made a point to include women from various socioeconomic groups and ethnic backgrounds—women whose voices often go unheard. You'll find out more about each of the women who inspired these stories in the Epilogue at the back of the book.

Since I started *Dancing in Combat Boots*, I have been elated to see more women embracing their stories from World War II. History tells us that pivotal time period fostered the modern civil rights, peace and women's movements, as well as the baby boom. And the women of World War II have lately launched a subtle movement in the schools, in library lecture rooms, in meeting rooms of veteran's organizations, in the memoir section of bookstores, to share more of their experiences. In so doing, our mothers and grandmothers are passing on their hard-earned wisdom. Their wartime struggles to balance work and family, independence and a happy marriage, self-fulfillment and a need to fit in, remain our struggles today.

Much as we'd like to believe (as these women so often expressed to me) that somehow the human race could move beyond war, what these women taught me is that what really matters is how we meet the challenges of a sometimes brutal world, how we retain our dignity, our compassion, and our values, and how we—as individuals—grow stronger. In our own "ordinary" lives, as we continue to push beyond our boundaries, it helps not only to know that someone else paved the way, but that given the right time and circumstance, any of us could do as these women did and rise above the roles society, nature and family expectations have set for us. We, too, could change the world without even realizing we were doing it.

A while back, I saw a colonel with all these bars on her shoulder, and I said, "Go girl! We made some tracks for you to walk in, though some of them were full of mud and sand. We were there and we laid the foundation."

— Judy Covington McKinnon

Dancing in Combat Boots

Kathryn

In Kathryn's dream, Le Havre is awash in moonlight,
nothing but steel forms of what had once been a city.
She'd entered France at that coastal village a month
earlier. Though it had not been her first taste of war,
for some reason, it is how the war has now come
to hold shape in her mind: that burned-out city,
bombed first by the Germans from land and then by
the Americans from the air.

She wakes in the French bricklayer's house in
Dijon, where she's billeted, still thinking she can
hear the minesweeper detonating mines in the
Channel. She lays very still, conserving heat and
energy, looking for patterns in the frost decorating
the inside of the window and thinking about Le
Havre. It helps sometimes to remember what she's
been through, what she's survived, as if the memories
mark steps already taken on a long journey home. It
is November, 1944.

Across the tiny room, Esther stirs, burrowing
deeper into her covers. She and Kathryn had been
two of the first Red Cross women to arrive in France,

and a dance had been held in their honor. They'd worn regulation slacks, blue-grey wool Eisenhower jackets and combat boots with stiff, high cuffs. By the end of the evening, the cuffs had turned their ankles bloody, but the dancing had kept them warm. Tonight they faced another long night of dancing, this time at the Christmas party at the club. Kathryn had suggested a nap might renew their energy, never imagining how much she'd want to go on sleeping.

"Do you know, Esther," Kathryn says with a yawn, "they say this is the coldest, snowiest winter Europe has seen in fifty years?"

"And for this I left Phoenix . . . Hey, Merry Christmas, Kat."

"Not quite yet."

"Well, Christmas Eve is the day that matters to my family," Esther explains. "It's when everyone travels to my mother's house, when the big meal is served, when Santa arrives."

Kathryn reflects on her parents and siblings. How far away they seem, not just in distance and time, but now also in experience. She starts to tell Esther about her family's traditions, but stops. After months of repeating her stories to soldier after soldier, she is sick of her own past. Sometimes she isn't even sure the stories are hers. The more she tells them, the more they seem to belong to someone else.

"I wish they'd let us grow our hair past our collars. It would keep us warmer," Esther says. "I know it sounds vain, but I used to consider my hair my best feature."

Kathryn always believed her best feature was her long neck until she realized it was not something men noticed. "Did I ever tell you I almost didn't make it over?" she says. "I was too skinny. I asked the doctor how to gain ten pounds in two weeks, and he said, 'Don't walk; take taxis. Eat big meals and two milkshakes a day, and drink an Ovaltine at night.'" Kathryn laughs. "I was a stuffed goose, but I made it."

They are both giggling now, and through the thin walls, their giggles tell the bricklayer's wife the American girls are up. They hear her opening and shutting cupboards in the kitchen.

Kathryn slips out of bed, shivering as her feet hit the cold floor. Not since she set foot in France has she felt warm. Just yesterday, she and Esther rode in the back of a jeep, a box of doughnuts between them to take to the men. By the time they reached the squadron, they were both so frozen they could barely bend. The men carried them into the building, sat them by the stove, and watched over them as they thawed. Finally, with fingers still tingling, the women set to work. Back at the club that afternoon—with the chill of the morning ride still locked in Kathryn's bones—a soldier said to her, "You talk smart for a Doughnut Dolly." It was all she could do not to slap him.

"I'm going downstairs to get us some tea," Kathryn says, pulling her overcoat on for extra warmth. In the kitchen, Kathryn puts two cups of tea on a serving tray. The bricklayer's wife adds a plate of bread and a couple of slices of cheese to the tray. "For you," she says. Kathryn protests. She can get food at the club. This family needs it more. But the lady insists. "*Joyeux Noel*," she says, kissing Kathryn's cheeks. She then makes her young sons do the same.

"Look what I've got, Esther," Kathryn chimes, but Esther is sitting at the edge of her bed, blouse half-buttoned, sobbing. Kathryn sets the plate down and lays a hand on her shoulder. "Is there anything I can do?" Esther shakes her head. Kathryn crosses quietly to her side of the room, keeping her back to Esther as she dresses. When she's ready, she sits on her bed looking at the floor, waiting. Eventually, Esther stops. She draws several deep breaths, then stands and finishes buttoning her uniform. She turns a weary smile on Kathryn. "You know what my perfect Christmas present would be, Kat?"

"What?"

"Never to see another doughnut."

"Now, Esther," Kathryn says, in the mock voice of their Red Cross trainer, "it's not about the doughnuts; it's about the men."

Kathryn offers her friend the bread, and they eat in silence, taking little pleasure in the food. Then quietly they gather their things and leave for the party.

Before the war, the train ride from Le Havre to Paris would have taken four hours; it had taken Kathryn's group four days. She had muddled through those days fighting a fever, determined to stay strong despite the cold and damp, watching the broken countryside crawl past through soot-covered windows. That's when the snow had started, and now here it was, Christmas Eve, and still it fell.

In Paris, she'd been assigned here, to Dijon, the headquarters for the 42nd Bomb Wing. She is working at the Red Cross club tonight, doing what she always does: serving drinks, coffee, candy; handing out cigarettes; talking to the GIs; dancing if the men want to. "Where're you from?" Kathryn starts, and eventually the man will realize she reminds him of a girl back home. "Tell me about her," she says.

The soldiers seem to take her in piece by piece. They watch her lips move when she speaks, her legs cross when she sits down, her chest rise when she sighs. They hold her close when they dance, smell her hair, stroke her back. For those few hours, she works to become everything they think they are fighting for.

As the evening wears on, her feet begin to hurt, and she needs to rest. She notices a young boy sitting by himself, a vacant chair beside him. "May I join you?"

"Yes, please," says the boy.

Across the room, GIs and Red Cross workers drift to the corners and the talk turns to war. When they've said too much, it will come back to happy memories and subtle innuendo. It's like that every night. When she first discovered she'd been assigned to "recreation services," Kathryn had worried. How was someone like her supposed to entertain battle-worn men? She'd never thought she was gifted at small talk or that she was a good dancer, and she hated playing cards. It was hard to believe she'd ever been concerned by things that had become second nature to her now.

"I'm Kathryn," she says to the boy.

"Andy Walker. Pleased to meet you, miss."

"Where are you from, Andy?"

"First Division. Came down from up north. It's snowing something fierce up there."

"No, I mean where in the States?"

"Oh! Oklahoma, miss." His eyes cloud. "The fightin's bad up North, have you heard? It's real bad."

"I know, Andy," she says, taking his hand. "But you're safe tonight. It's Christmas."

He wipes his nose on his sleeve. "You remind me of my big sis," he says. "Can I show you a picture?" He's nineteen, and his pictures are of the farm he left behind and his family—his sister, his dad, and his mother, a drawn-looking woman whose look of worry seems to weigh heavily on her son.

"Now, tell me about you," he says.

"I really should talk to some of these other men."

"Please. Just tell me where you're from."

She catches sight of Esther standing among a handful of GIs, one hand on her hip, the other against a soldier's chest. She's chastising him, but smiling at the same time. The other men can't seem to stand close enough.

"I was born in Bethel, Ohio. Small town," Kathryn says. "My father owned a shoe factory. When I was eight, we moved to Cincinnati. I had a lovely childhood—like yours on the farm."

She does not tell him about her degree from Simmons College in Boston, nor that she worked for a New York ad agency writing travel columns until the war shut down the travel industry. She does not let on that when her own brave mother found out she'd be shipping overseas, she had simply replied, "I wish I was younger." What he needs to know is that she's like him, so that's what she tells him.

"You okay now, Andy? I should mingle."

"Wait," he says. "I want to give you something—a present." He's rifling through his pockets.

"You don't need to give me anything."

"Please wait," he says. "I have a pack of gum here somewhere. Here it is!" When he holds out his gift, Andy realizes the pack contains only one piece of gum. "I'm sorry," he says. "I thought it was full." He throws it to the floor. Kathryn picks it up and removes the last stick of gum. She takes Andy's hand and holds on even when his grip hurts her fingers. "Thank you, Andy. I thought I wouldn't be getting any presents this year. This means a lot."

The boy beams and lets go of her hand. He remembers his manners and stands when she stands. He thanks her for talking to him and says he'll look her up in Cincinnati after the war. If every soldier who has made that promise actually follows through, what a fine parade that will be, Kathryn thinks. As she goes to find Esther, she tucks the stick of gum into her pocket.

The men are gone, and the women are finished with cleanup. Five of them gather around a table, cups of coffee warming their hands. They complain about aching feet and sore backs and wave away yawns, but no one rises to leave. Rumors are circulating they'll be moving out soon. This is their last chance to focus on each other for a change.

Kathryn has been quiet for most of the conversation, but the coffee is giving her a second wind, just when the others are winding down. "We came over on the *Argentina*, right along with the troops," she begins. "We traveled for two weeks in a convoy of fifty-four ships, with the *Argentina* in the lead. They dropped depth charges on enemy subs while we were on board, and still I didn't grasp that I was in the war."

"What? There's a war on?" Esther jokes, and everyone laughs.

Kathryn continues, "The transport commander didn't like having women aboard, but he loved to play bridge, so we assigned three of our best bridge players to play with him every evening. We joined the choir, worked on the ship's newspaper, asked for classes in military procedure, held a couple of dances on deck. Do you know, for that first dance, the officers had to assign sailors to come? The second dance, they had to fight them off." She crosses her arms and leans back. "Well, when we came into Liverpool, that commander announced over the PA system that we'd done an outstanding job. Said he was proud to have us aboard."

The women sigh and shake their heads. It has always been a man's world—now more than ever.

"So, when did it feel like war to you?" Esther asks.

Visions of Le Havre cross Kathryn's mind, but the hour is late, and the situation calls for levity. She chooses this story instead: "I was billeted on Charles Street in London, where the buzz bombs fell. Now, if you heard the motor cut off, the bomb was going to drop, and it was going to blow up a whole block." A girl named Jane turns away. She too had been billeted on Charles Street. "The Londoners would hear that sound and dive headfirst into the gutter or an areaway leading to a basement, without the least embarrassment. I'd have felt ridiculous doing that."

"You'd have felt worse getting hit by shrapnel," Jane says.

Kathryn ignores her. "At night you'd see people dressed in pajamas and robes walking down the street toward the shelter. Not me," Kathryn says. "I'd rather die in the open."

"You might still get your wish."

"So, one night I asked the fire warden, 'What do I do if I'm in the bathtub and the bombs fall?' 'Girlie,' the old gentleman said, 'you don't need to worry about that. If one falls near, it'll blow your clothes off anyway.'"

They all laugh, even Jane, just a little, and the commotion brings in the MPs who've been assigned to see them home. They push back from the table, hugging each other, and carry cups and cigarette butts to the sink.

"Oh, that stench of doughnuts," Esther groans. "Will we ever get it out of our clothes?"

"It's not about the doughnuts," Kathryn says, and in unison, she and Esther recite, "it's about the men."

Shortly after Christmas, Kathryn and Esther are sent to join the 44th Infantry Division at the front. But the concept of "the front" is difficult to grasp. Everything is fluid motion. At times, it is explained to them, they might actually be behind enemy lines and not know it. "If you are taken prisoner, you are to assume the rank of second lieutenant," an officer reminds them. "According to the Geneva Convention, officers should receive better treatment. Then again," he says, wincing, "since you're civilians, we can't issue you guns." To him, this must seem especially distressing. A soldier without his gun is nothing; he's a marked man. But to Kathryn, it's a relief not to carry a weapon. She didn't join this war to kill anyone. She joined because sewing baby clothes and layettes for civilian relief, knitting sweaters and mittens for the military and rolling bandages for the Red Cross had not seemed enough. She joined because it made her angry to see young men who'd been drafted trying to buy commissions to be officers or neighbors hoarding sugar to sell on the black market. She went to war because her parents had raised her to believe that those more fortunate were obliged to give back. And when the military wouldn't take her because of her bad eyes, she turned to the

Red Cross. She came to Europe to serve, not to kill, and maybe, like most who believe they are in the right, she thought that would keep her safe.

When the women arrive at the front, the chief personnel officer takes them to task. "You are not to be heroines," he says in a voice as stern as a schoolmaster's. "You are to do exactly as you're told. You are to go no farther forward than the command tells you. If you come under attack, there will be somebody assigned to take you to a foxhole, and you are to stay there until they tell you to get out. Do I make myself understood?" He does.

The women are given a two-and-a-half-ton truck to turn into a clubmobile. It is nothing compared to the fully equipped clubmobiles they had in England. Those had been converted buses with their front sections turned into kitchens boasting coffee urns, doughnut machines and mixer bowls, and the back sections serving as lounges where the men could talk and read magazines. They'd had PA systems for playing records, and the men had clambered to get aboard. Then again, they'd feel the same way about this broken-down truck. Kathryn is sure of that and she's right, of course. The first doughnut she makes is taken and framed by the men. They promise to keep it with them throughout the war.

Eventually Kathryn and the others jump off into Germany. Sometimes the women sleep in tents, sometimes in houses in the towns. It is early spring 1945, and still the snow falls lightly. One morning, they are walking back from the quartermaster's tent

when a plane flies in low from the North. They
hear it before they see it. German planes have been
flying over, scouting for convoys. The girls have
learned not to count on the red cross painted on the
clubmobile or on their own, recognizable uniforms
for protection. The Germans are fond of strafing
anything that moves. Kathryn and Esther sprint for
cover, making lovely targets as they streak across the
snow toward the woods. In the safety of the trees,
they laugh about their luck, until the fear catches
up to them and sends them briefly into each other's
arms.

They pull apart, still holding hands.

"You okay?"

"Yeah. You?"

Esther begins to shake. Kathryn brushes snow off
a fallen log and says, "Sit here. Catch your breath."

"Goddamn Germans."

"Esther! What would your mother say?"

"She'd tell me to get home this instant. If I had any
sense, that's exactly what I'd do."

"Sense? There's no sense in wartime. We're moving
forward, Esther. I expect we'll see more of this, and
God knows what else."

Kathryn takes a few steps to the edge of the
clearing and peers across the field toward camp. A
gasoline barrel is burning and men are shouting, but
otherwise the scene is still.

"Why don't you ever seem afraid?" Esther says.

"Don't be foolish. Didn't you see me a moment
ago? Do you think I could run that fast if I wasn't

scared to death?"

"But look at you now. And look at me. Aren't you scared of dying?"

"We're too young to die," Kathryn quips, but a vision of Andy Walker's boyish smile flicks through her mind. He could be dead already, his farm-wife mother watching down the road for his casket to arrive. Kathryn turns her eyes toward the snow-grey sky and watches snowflakes catch in the branches of the tree. In all these weeks, she has not yet found a way to put into words how she feels. Not even in her letters home can she explain to her mother exactly why she shouldn't worry. She just knows she shouldn't.

But Esther is waiting for an answer. "We're not at war with anyone, Esther. Not truly. Not like them." She nods toward the camp. "We could run away anytime we wanted to. You could go home tomorrow, and it wouldn't hurt a soul. Knowing I'm where I asked to be—I don't know—it makes a difference somehow."

Esther wraps her arms tightly around herself and begins to rock. "Can't stop my teeth from chattering."

"Hold on. I've got something that might help. It's probably a bit stale, though."

"Gum? I thought you hated gum."

"I do. It was a gift." The camp is moving now, men rushing to put things back in order, calling to each other for help or cigarettes or clarification of orders, gloating over the inaccuracy of German gunners. Above the noise, Kathryn hears someone calling their names. She watches a few soldiers circle the clubmobile, looking for damage or signs of the women. She waves Esther over to see.

"It's like having fifteen thousand big brothers, isn't it?" Esther says.

"It is."

"I'm sorry I lost my composure, Kat."

"But look at you now, Esther. It's a wonder, isn't it? How we keep pulling ourselves together." She puts an arm around Esther and pulls her in close. "You know what I think? I think we're good at what we do. We play our roles well, but we're stronger than those boys think. Maybe someday they'll realize that." She gives Esther's shoulder a firm squeeze. "But I don't suppose they need to know it yet. We should get back before they start to worry."

As the women step together into the field, several soldiers run to meet them, guns in hand, eyes scouring the woods for danger. Kathryn recognizes one of the GIs. He's the one who told her she talked smart for a Doughnut Dolly. She hesitates for a second, throwing Esther an incredulous glance, then takes the arm he offers and lets him lead her through the heavy snow.

The Enemy You Know

Charlotte

It had been three weeks and three days since Charlotte had received a letter from Henry. The girls in the carpool told her to get some sleep, but she no longer felt secure alone in her bed. At the office, she drank glass after glass of water and still her throat felt dry. She couldn't shake the image of Henry lifted high in the air, his clothes blown backward, his gun dropping from his hand, his eyes shut tight against the blast. "Soldiers are nothin' but cannon fodder," her uncle used to say. Tears gathered again. There was no stopping them anymore.

"Now, Charlotte," Bernice said. "You'll hear from him soon. Don't he always write? Lot better than my Frank."

Charlotte pulled a handkerchief from her sleeve. "Big baby, that's what I am. Trained into me from birth. Youngest of ten, you know."

Bernice smiled. "Finished that inventory yet?"

"Just about."

"Well, bring it over when you're done." Bernice turned back toward her desk. A German prisoner assigned to the office took a broom from the storage closet and began to sweep the concrete floor. "Whatcha lookin' at, boy?" Bernice snapped. "Keep your eyes on your work."

The prisoner lowered his head and angled his broom into a corner. The *PW* on the back of his shirt ruffled each time he shifted his arms. Closer to this boy's homeland, in the fields of France, Henry was working in a prisoner of war camp too. He was assigned to a quartermaster unit there just as she was here in Colorado, not so much a coincidence, in her mind, as further proof they were meant to be together.

"Have you noticed," she called to Bernice, "how the men aren't just their names anymore? Now they're 'my Frank' or 'my Robert.' You suppose we think if we take possession of them they can't get hurt without our permission?"

"Okay, college girl. Whatever you say."

Charlotte noticed the German boy glance up at her. "I didn't actually go to college," she said to him. "I was the first in my family to graduate high school, though. I had a scholarship to a business school, but my dad took sick, and it fell to me to care for him."

"Whatcha talkin' to him for? He don't even know what you're sayin.'"

But Charlotte wasn't so sure. She thought she saw him smile.

Bernice shook her head at both of them. After her husband enlisted, Bernice moved back to the family farm, but she drove into the town of Greeley

each day to pick up Charlotte and four other girls to
bring them to Camp 202. Farm rations allowed for
extra gasoline, so Bernice insisted she was only doing
her part, but Charlotte knew it was the first time
her friend had spent so much time in the company
of women. For all her gruffness, it was clear Bernice
missed her husband just like everyone else in that car.
Each morning she'd pull up in her enormous Buick,
and Charlotte would crawl in back with two other
women. She'd bounce one of Ruby's infant twins on
her lap as Bernice grumbled about the extra effort it
took to get those darn kids to the sitter's. Ruby always
sat up front next to Bernice so she could put her arm
around her shoulder and tell her what a good egg she
was, while her babies fussed in someone else's care.
There were days Charlotte wished she and Henry
had not made a point of putting off children until
after the war. She wondered if a child would make
her feel closer to Henry. Then she remembered that if
he never came home, there would be no child . . . ever.
Now in the car, she reached over and took one of the
twins onto her lap.

On the way to camp, they passed Bernice's
farm. Her father and older brother were already
in the fields. Her younger brother and most of the
field hands had succumbed to the lure of battle,
so Bernice's farm, like many others, now relied on
POW labor, one of the reasons many of the camps
were located in rural areas. This morning, a farmer's
pickup passed, German POWs peering out between
the sideboards, and the women went quiet. For

eight hours a day they looked at these same men but through the panels of the hogwire fence. That is how they'd come to know them. To see them huddled in the back of a pickup headed for the fields made them look a little too much like the boys round here.

Charlotte dropped her pencil. It was not yet noon, and already it had been a long day. She'd risen early to bathe her mother, fix breakfast, make a pie for dinner, and clean up the dishes. And she'd written to Henry, of course, as she did every morning, though sometimes it took her two days to finish a letter.

"How is it you got so much to say?" her mother would ask from beneath her blankets. "Is your life so interesting these days?"

"Oh, I can always talk to Henry. He never has minded like some men do." It was difficult, though, having to keep most of the information about her days at the camp to herself for fear of the censors and, for Henry's sake, playing down her mother's illness, the repairs on the house that weren't getting done, her own relentless fears about what she would do if he didn't come home. She couldn't burden him with that, but neither could she keep from telling him how much she missed him every hour of every day.

Charlotte had met Henry at a Valentine's Day dance when she was seventeen. He was twenty, stocky and handsome, with dark, close-cut hair and a shy smile. He was already in the service at Fitzsimons Army Hospital in Denver, and she'd be lying if she said his uniform didn't catch her eye. Course, it never occurred to her then how much that uniform would haunt her dreams, how often she'd wish he didn't have to wear it. When the war started, she was sure they'd take Henry overseas right away, but he was granted a reprieve. He was classified an essential worker at the commissary, and there was no one to replace him. Charlotte got a job at Fitzsimons too, trying not to notice the sick and wounded soldiers arriving from battlefields all over the world or how the towns around Denver were emptying of young men. Every day she thanked God that Henry was right there with her.

Sixteen months after they married, the war caught up to them. Returning from a bus trip, they found Henry's orders to leave for overseas that very day. There were new clothes to be issued, shots to get, good-byes to say. That night he left, and Charlotte stood on the platform wondering how life could turn upside down in a matter of hours. To her, the train's sleek, black engine resembled a hearse. As soon as Henry left, there was always some part of Charlotte that felt knotted or tensed or tight; yet inside she felt hollow. She went home to Greeley, to her ailing parents and a transfer to the 320-acre prisoner of war camp outside of town.

So it could not be said she didn't understand the restlessness she saw in the prisoners' eyes, or the heavy shuffle of their steps. When everything you care about has been taken from you, you want to act out and give up all at once. But at least she was home. As she leaned against the window, watching some German prisoners rehearse a scene for a play,

she marveled again at their ability to sing under such
circumstances, to fashion furniture out of cardboard
boxes, to work ten hours in the fields, arriving back at
camp tired and hungry but with little complaint. Back
in '43, when Italians also were held here, before Italy
switched sides and they were sent home, Bernice said
there had been laughter. But the Germans were more
serious. There would be no heroes' welcomes for them
when they got home. They were a conquered army,
and they knew it. Perhaps there was nothing left to
laugh about.

"Charlotte, you got that inventory yet?"

"Sorry, Bernice. It's right here."

Three weeks and four days and still nothing.
Charlotte had barely slept last night. She'd lain awake
listening to her mother's raspy breathing, the bump
and hiss of the radiator, a branch scraping the side
of the house. She'd risen early to pace and pray and
promise God that if she got a letter today, she'd put
an extra offering in the basket on Sunday. It had been
a relief to get into that Buick this morning, to take
one of the twins in her arms and nuzzle his neck, to
hear the confident chatter of the women, the way they
teased her about her fear. "When you see an officer
coming up your steps with a solemn look, that's when
you gotta worry," Bernice said. "Anyone see any officers
round here?"

The baby wiggled in Charlotte's arms, patting her
cheeks with both his hands. He wanted to play peek-

a-boo, and Charlotte was his favorite. She smiled
and covered her face. When her hands flew apart, he
laughed harder than expected, and everyone laughed
with him. From the front seat, Ruby threw Charlotte
a smile. The autumn sun shone clear and bright
across the Colorado plains. By the time she reached
the camp, the throbbing in her temples had begun
to subside and by afternoon she began humming
as she stuffed a piece of paper into the Underwood
typewriter. The German boy was washing windows.
"I know this song," he said, humming along with her
for a moment.

"That's right," she said. "Very good."

The boy jumped down off his stool, tossing the
wet rag in the bucket. "This is German song."

"I suppose it is. My mother taught it to me."

"You speak German, *ja*? So does she." He nodded
toward Bernice's desk.

"Well, plenty of folks round here speak German.
You know why that is, don't you?"

The boy took another step forward, wiping his
wet hands on his uniform. There was an eagerness in
him that Charlotte couldn't help but like. If this war
hadn't come along, she could picture him sitting in
a university in Munich or Berlin, hanging on some
professor's every word. She wondered if he longed
for that other life while he pushed the broom around
the office or topped sugar beets in the fields. She
wondered if he had a girl back home who waited for
letters from him. Charlotte checked out the window
for Bernice but saw only a guard tossing a ball back

over the twelve-foot fence.

"Most folks round here are what we call Germans from Russia. Originally our people came from Germany. Then Catherine the Great put out a call for farmers to build up the Volga region, and we went. Later, when things went wrong for us in Russia, we settled here in Weld County. When I was small, I spoke nothing but German. Then I went to school, and they told us to speak English. I guess it slips out once in a while, though. Is that how you knew?"

The boy nodded. "Some of the farmers say German to us. Some women cook food for us."

"Yes, well, they're not supposed to do that."

"No, is *gut*, is *gut*. Make us think of home." The boy took another tentative step toward her desk. He laid two fingers gently atop the picture of Henry looking sharp in his army uniform. "And your husband is German too?"

Charlotte looked from the fingers that draped her husband's picture to the other hand that hung limp at the boy's side. At some point, those slender hands had gripped the stock of a rifle that might have been pointed at Henry, or Bernice's husband, or Ruby's. There may have been dirt beneath his fingernails from crawling toward a sleeping American squadron, or tobacco stains on his fingers from cigarettes stolen off a dead GI. She yanked the picture away. "Don't ever touch this again," she said, "Get back to work now. Go on."

Their eyes locked for a moment, then he backed away. He could not have been more than twenty years

old. Just a boy, she told herself, until she remembered
she was only twenty-two. In another time and place,
she could have been his favorite sister or the girl he
left behind. They had both lost so much, but whose
fault was that? They should ask themselves that, she
thought, as she glanced out her window toward the
prisoners milling around behind the fence, nearly
three thousand of them in all. Ask themselves whose
fault it is they are here and our boys are there. Ask
me why I should feel sorry for them, for the meals
we provide, the 80 cents a day they are paid for their
farm labor, the clothing and shelter and medical care.
If my husband winds up in one of their camps, will
he get as much?

Ruby was now standing where the boy had been,
snapping her fingers to get Charlotte's attention.
"Didn't your mother ever caution you about worry
lines?"

Charlotte looked past her. The prisoner's bucket
and stool were still there, but he was gone.

"Why do so few of them try to escape?" Charlotte
said. "If it were you, wouldn't you at least try to get
home?"

"And where would I go? Would I just walk back to
Germany?"

"Look at them, though. Riding out the war in
peace."

"They've lost their freedom, Charlotte. They're
sitting behind that fence, going mad with boredom.
I'd hardly call that peace."

"Well, they look like they've got it pretty good to

me."

"It's only been three weeks since you've heard
from him, Charlotte. You've got to stop assuming
the worst." She came around the desk and pulled one
of the pins from Charlotte's hair, holding it between
her teeth as she twisted the errant hairs back into
place. "The war's winding down. Pretty soon they'll
ship these men back where they came from, and this
camp will go to field again. This whole thing will be a
memory. You just have to hang in there."

"You're right. It doesn't help to cry about it."

"Oh, you can cry if you want. We all do
sometimes."

Charlotte was walking back the next day from lunch
at the officers' club when she noticed a shift in the
prisoners even before she heard the truck. Men who
had gathered to talk or play cards or read aloud to one
another were heading toward the fence. Others were
running in from the soccer field and the horseshoe
pit. Charlotte watched the truck roll past the two
stone pillars that marked the entrance to the camp.
By now, the incarcerated POWs were pressed up
tight against the fence, their fingers gripping the wire.
This new shipment of men had come straight from
the heart of war, carted halfway across the world
to Greeley by ship and then by train. They were
bedraggled and sickly, and their eyes flicked nervously
as they took in this new place through the slats in the
truck. The men inside the camp started their chorus,

which set the dogs barking, which brought the guards
in closer. As the new group of soldiers was led past
the fence, the men inside shouted names of towns
and family members, tossed sticks of gum and pieces
of paper through the fence with addresses written on
them, looking for anyone from home.

Bernice came up behind Charlotte. "Get a load of
this lot."

"Look, Bernice. By the fence."

Two men were crying and grasping at each other's
clothing, pulling each other close through the wire.
Charlotte rose up on her toes to see better. As the
guards prodded them forward, the new batch of
prisoners dragged their feet, looking back over their
shoulders at the weeping men while the POWs
inside the camp backed off, leaving a pocket of space
around them. Charlotte listened hard.

"Father and son?" she said. "Is that what they're
saying?"

"That's it. Not much of a homecoming, huh?"

Charlotte felt a tear slide down her cheek. Three
weeks and five days and still no word. "Better than no
homecoming at all."

As the guards led the father away from the son,
the older man covered his face with his hands while
the younger one shoved his way toward the prisoner
entrance to meet his father. Charlotte watched the
camp POWs drift back toward the fence, toward the
now-empty truck. They were silent and still.

"Come back inside," Bernice said. "While you're
gawking at them, they're gawking at you."

Just then, Charlotte noticed the German boy who cleaned the office standing several feet away, watching her. She wiped the tears from her cheek as she held his gaze. When he finally moved to pass her, she reached out and touched his arm.

Except for a twitch in his right cheek, the boy showed no emotion, but his eyes fixed on her hand. He didn't dare touch her, not with the guards so close, but he looked up and nodded.

Charlotte did not follow him back inside. Not yet. Beyond the tree-lined gravel roads of the camp, beyond the neat rows of tan prison barracks, the theater, the bakery, the watchtowers with their searchlights and machine guns, Longs Peak loomed in the distance, constant and serene. Beyond that, only God knew.

An officer approached, waving a count of the new prisoners. With a sigh, Charlotte followed him into the office, grateful for the distraction the work would bring. The women got busy issuing forest-green uniforms, overcoats, underwear, soap and toilet paper to the new arrivals while the German boy replaced the bucket in the storage closet. Bernice swiveled sharply in her chair, banging her knee on the desk. "*Das war dumm*," she said under her breath, and then to the boy, "Now what're you looking at?" He closed the closet door and turned to leave. As he passed Charlotte, she saw him smile.

Las Estrellas de Oro

Elena

¡*Ay!* It's hot in the store today. Reminds me of my last summer in Mexico, when I was five. And there she is in the corner, thinking I can't see her. Thinking I can't *feel* what she is doing. She doesn't know about this instinct I've developed, but she also doesn't know I understand. These ladies are not thieves, just mothers with too many children who haven't learned to spread out their ration points. She sticks a two-pound bag of sugar into her bloomers, and I shake my head but say nothing. When she comes to the counter with her other goods, I simply charge her for the sugar. She looks as if the shame will kill her. I offer her son a candy. It is not rationed. I can hand it out as I please.

Mexico. My only real memories are of the heat and the way my older sisters held their heads high when they walked along the boardwalks, the way my brothers talked of the things they would do, the fine girls they would marry, as they stocked shelves in my father's dry goods store. They belonged in a place like this, like San Antonio, far from the dust and poverty and violence of Saltillo, and they knew it even then.

America is our home now, and we never complain.
Our mother's eyes no longer burn with worry.

A colored kid comes in. He calls me Boss Lady,
and I laugh. I'm 25 years old. By now, the only people
I should be bossing are my own *niños*. But the war
has changed things. I will not marry until it is over.
Tomás understands that. He's stationed at Camp
Hood, and he knows I love him, but he won't ask
me to walk away from the store. He accepts I will
not be one of those soldiers' wives following her
husband from base to base, dumped in some old,
ugly place with bad plumbing and windows that
won't close. And I'm sure not going to be one of those
heartbroken ladies with a kid or two and a husband
off at war. My brother Alejandro is in Detroit
working for the defense industry. He tells me I
should join him. He tells me about the money I could
make, but my place is here. Besides, how could I leave
my *mamá*?

I thought my brother Eduardo was *loco* when he
volunteered *me* to run his store after he joined the
Navy. "But, Eddie," I said, "I have no experience."

"Oh, you'll do all right," he said.

And I have. I'll stay till the end of the war, till
Eddie comes back.

I do all the buying and selling and take care of the
ration points. I make good money, forty-five dollars
a week, but we're not getting rich. The government
won't let us. Just yesterday, a woman planning her
daughter's *quinceañera* begged me to sell her extra
sugar under the counter. She had the money, she said.

"You have plenty of food in this store," she said. "It's not right for you not to share."

"And what if I get caught?" I said. "We'd lose our permit. Borrow some sugar from your neighbor. Use molasses. Don't ask me this again."

Old Señor Zamora frowned when he heard how I had spoken to her. There are those in the neighborhood who think a young woman shouldn't hold such a high post. But I believe people will take you for how you behave. I've always been seen as a lady. Like my sisters, I hold my head high. It's a plus to have that respect, to have the respect shown our family.

When Eddie married, my father gave him fifty dollars worth of merchandise to start his own grocery store. Eddie was ambitious. He had only half a dozen cans of sardines to start out, yet he had the nerve to put out flyers saying they were on sale. That half-dozen sold, and he dashed to the wholesale house to get more. He did the same with canned milk and sugar. When pinto beans were in season, he bought three times more than would sell, so when the other stores ran out, he'd still have some. Now ours is one of the biggest stores in the city, but I still greet most everyone by name.

The government inspector will show up any day now, but I'm not worried. There's a new coat of paint on the walls. The shelves are clean, and the accounting and rationing books are in order. He will mark our store perfect condition again, and I will display his report with a swell of pride. Eddie's wife

is in the back, tending to her seven children, and I'm
grateful that, as much as there is to be done today, as
humid as it is, as bad as my feet hurt, at least I'm not
standing in her shoes.

Most days I work from seven to seven, but not
today, *gracias a Dios*. We close early on Thursdays
because the downtown stores stay open till nine.
This is the day I usually do my shopping, the day
I go to the movies or my sewing club. We eat *pan
dulce* and embroider pillowcases and linens for our
future, for the days when we will marry our boys. On
Thursday nights, I get away from this place, from the
responsibilities and the feeling of being so tied down.

This is what I'm looking forward to as I go to the
window to straighten the blue star that hangs there
for our Eddie. Outside, the Martinez girls skip rope
on the sidewalk. They are calling to me to come out
and count for them. What they really hope is that I
will jump. I laugh and tell them it's too hot today, that
I want to stay inside by the fan, but they plead with
me from the doorway. "Run down to the corner and
look for Manuel's truck," I tell them. "Tell me when
he's coming, and I'll give you a piece of *leche quemada*.
My sister and her husband have run out of canned
milk at their store, and I have told them they can have
some of mine. I'm hoping Manuel will take a look at
the fan while he's here. It has stopped moving back
and forth. But before the girls can run off, there is a
loud noise, like the buzz of an insect near your ear.
The girls point toward the sky. "*Señorita Vallejo*," they
say. "*¡Mira!*" I follow their tiny fingers to a place where

a column of smoke rises. In an instant, I have the older girl's shoulders between my hands.

"What did you see, Carolina?"

"A plane," she says. "It went down behind that tall tree."

"Stay here," I tell her. "Watch the store for me."

I should not leave, of course, not without calling for my sister-in-law, at least, but I have to see it. I have to feel this war that has wrapped around me like an old man's *serape* but not yet touched me. I want to feel as though there is something I can do about it. We are surrounded by bases—Fort Sam Houston, Randolph Air Force Base, Kelly, Stinson Field. Navy seamen visit from Corpus Christi. We know them all, the soldiers, the airmen, the sailors. We dance with them at the USO near the Alamo. We sacrifice for them, giving up our nylon stockings for their parachutes, wearing the same shoes day after day, cutting the material for our dresses short so they have enough fabric for their uniforms. Sometimes, though, like air or the spirit of God, you can be surrounded by something and still have to work to believe it's real.

Before I reach the crash site, I hear the news from the neighbors. An aviator on a training mission lost control of his plane. I see one piece of his body here, another there, and I cover my eyes and turn away. This I should not see. This was a man, someone's son and brother. *Mamá* would say I should not have come. This is none of my business. But now that I'm here, I cannot move. I stand with the women, weeping and praying to Our Lady as some of the

men put the body back together while others try
to shield us from the scene already burned into our
memories. Señora Cruz hands the men her *rebozo*
and they cover the body with her shawl. Señora
Cruz is known for her shawls. The women in the
neighborhood come to her for advice or ask her to
make special *rebozos* for their daughters. We have
given this young man the best we can offer, and that
finally loosens the bonds of our grief.

I need to get back to the store, but my feet will
not hurry, and my mind will not let go of the thought
that now a mother or young sweetheart will replace
her blue star with a gold one. I cry as I walk down my
street because I have failed before to notice just how
many gold stars there are in the windows of my little
neighborhood. I was foolish to think I could help
that boy, that I could somehow touch this distant
war. Its true horror dances out of reach, like an evil
spirit, taunting us.

The Martinez girls are full of questions when I
return, but they are too young to hear such things, so
I shoo them away. I remind myself there is work to
do before closing, that I can best honor the ones who
die by doing my part.

My friend from Connecticut wrote once to
complain, "There are no men here anymore. You have
them all in San Antonio." I think about that aviator
and wonder if he could have been a Connecticut boy.
Until today, I didn't think much about where these
young men came from or where they went when they
left us. Of course, I knew most were here for only a

short time, that it was our duty to entertain them, to
see them off well, but I never let myself imagine what
happened next.

Tonight I will not go to my sewing club. I will say
a rosary for that pilot and his family instead. I will
remind God that I have already lost one brother to
leukemia, another to an accident, and ask Him to
please spare Eddie, to keep Tomás at Camp Hood
and let no other woman tempt him. I will thank Him
for my many blessings and ask Him to forgive my
selfish heart.

I had thought we were such a powerful country
that this war would be over in a month. Now it is
dragging on into years. I have been waiting for the
war to end so I can start my life, a life with Tomás.
Now I realize *ésta es mi vida*, this *is* my life. It is true
I am not where I expected to be, not even where I
always want to be, but coming home from that crash
today, seeing the door to the store standing open, my
sister-in-law with the baby on her hip, the customers
waiting patiently at the counter, I know I am where I
need to be. God has reminded me of that.

Black Smoke Rising

Marjorie

It's not that some of us didn't think there could be a
war or that it would start in the Pacific; we just never
believed it would begin here. Before last Sunday,
Wayne and I lived in a newly built apartment at the
far end of Hickam Field with only a fence between
us and Pearl Harbor. Before Sunday, our biggest
decision of an evening was whether to stay on base
and go bowling or drive into town to dance. Back
then, I taught third grade at a private school for
military parents whose primary concern was not an
invasion, but their children picking up pidgin English
from the Hawaiians. Wayne was an aircraft mechanic
and a staff sergeant in the army. Now he's a soldier—
a real one.

Last Saturday evening our neighbor Don barreled
through our front door to tell us the latest alert had
just been lifted. After two weeks of confinement to
the base, we were finally free. Wayne and I dumped
our dinner dishes in the sink and ran to the car,
laughing when I tripped over our short-haired terrier,
Buddy, who'd wound his leash around my legs in

his excitement. We spent the evening playing cards at Stan and Sylvia's house near Diamond Head. "Welcome, newlyweds," Stan had said, knowing I feel too old at twenty-seven for such a frivolous term. But Stan served his famous pineapple cocktails and Sylvia her crabmeat canapés, and I paid Stan back by beating him soundly at gin. Coming home late that night, we flung our clothes over the chair and fell into bed, planning to sleep late. I wonder now if I'll ever sleep that soundly again.

———

To wake to the sound of airplanes was nothing unusual. Just part of life on the base, where the military dictated everything we experienced. But that morning there was something different in the low-flying roar of the engines. That day the planes came directly over our apartment, shaking our little bedroom. "Boy, the navy is really practicing today," I said hopefully, but Wayne was already crawling over me toward the window.

I joined him in time to see a plane go screaming past, so close I could see the pilot's face turned slightly in our direction, his goggles up on his forehead instead of over his eyes, his face unmistakably Oriental.

"That's a bomber. Look, the Rising Sun!" Wayne pointed out the flaming orange insignia just behind the wing.

In the yard, Buddy leaped up on his doghouse and barked fiercely at the monsters.

Oh my God, I thought, but I couldn't say it. My mouth felt full of straw.

"Hurry!" Wayne shouted, as off in the direction of Pearl the first bombs hit. Buddy's bark changed to an anguished howl. I yanked my dress over my head, slipping into my pumps at the same time. Wayne pulled me down the stairs and across the kitchen. I had just enough time to grab my purse and cast a glance at those dishes in the sink, wondering if I'd ever see this place again.

In the front yard, Don stood with his arm around Carol. Baby Ann wailed in Carol's arms and kicked her tiny feet, while four-year-old Timmy pressed his hands to his ears. Over Pearl and Hickam, black smoke was rising.

"They're hitting the hangars," Don said.

"We've got to move the planes," Wayne shouted.

"What should we do, Wayne?" I asked, knowing full well what his answer would be.

"Get off the base, Marjorie. Now!"

I swept up Timmy as Wayne and Don led the way around the building toward the cars parked out back. The dust and smoke choked us, settling on our bare arms and faces. When the ground shook, it was like walking on ice skates.

"Wayne!" I cried as he reached our Ford.

He came back, kissed me hard and said, "Don't worry."

I watched him get into our car, our eyes meeting for just a moment before he threw a look over his shoulder and backed the car out of the lot. As I

lowered Timmy into the backseat of Carol's car, she
tried to hand me the baby. "Just a minute!" I rushed
over to Buddy. In his panic, he snapped at me, and
I gave up grabbing for his collar and pulled up the
stake, releasing his leash. I called to him, but he tore
off into the bushes.

"Leave him!" Carol screamed, shoving Ann into
my arms and running around to the driver's seat,
scraping her leg on the fender as she went. From
the front of the Dodge we cooed comforts to the
children, glancing off to the right, where Pearl
Harbor burned, where our husbands were now
headed. Had it not been for Ann digging her tiny
fingernails into my forearm, I might have jumped
from the car. I turned the baby toward me, and her
clear blue eyes fixed on mine as she clung to the
bodice of my dress. I shushed her gently as we sped
through the base gate.

As we flew down the highway, we left the smoke
and sirens behind us, but not the shock. It was there
in the tears that slid down Carol's cheeks and the
way she hunched over the steering wheel. I felt it in
my chest, where my lungs clung too tightly to each
breath. I closed my eyes for just a moment. When
I was a child, my family had wandered the country
like nomads, often living out of our car as my father
sought work in those troubled times. Crowded into
that Model T between my brothers and sister, I
discovered that when you close your eyes in a moving
car, the rattle in your bones feels the same whether
the road is in Kansas or Kentucky. With my eyes

closed now, I could take myself back to the highway
heading to the primary school in Los Angeles where
I'd served as principal. Back then, I'd been too busy
to believe there could ever be a man like Wayne
who could make me walk away from my career or a
place like Hawaii that could make me abandon the
stable home I'd finally established for myself. Now,
everything was changing again.

When the Dodge hit a pothole, the baby startled,
and my breath released. I glanced at Carol, who was
shaking her head.

"Where should I go, Margie? I don't know where
to go."

"Head for town," I said, holding the baby closer.
Timmy stood behind us, his elbows draped over the
bench seat, his hands ready to cover his ears again.
"Timmy," I said in my best teaching voice, "tell me
about swimming yesterday. Did you find me a good
shell at the beach?"

Timmy lowered his hands. "I found a dead fish
and I put it on our blanket and Mama said *damn*."

"Timmy!" his mother cried, but I patted his arm
and gave him a smile. Just then, a young Oriental
woman appeared by the roadside ahead. She was
holding hands with a little boy about Timmy's age.
She turned and looked straight into our windshield,
and when she saw my smile, she must have assumed
it was for her because she raised a timid hand.

"Should I stop?" Carol asked.

"Yes. I'll get in back with Timmy." I reached for the
door handle, afraid if I didn't, Carol might not find

the courage to help.

When the car stopped, the young mother scooted into the front seat, settling her son on her lap. "*Arigato gozaimasu*," she mumbled, and then we knew for certain she was Japanese and not Chinese or Filipina. None of us spoke, though her son made clucking noises at Timmy, trying to engage him in play. But Timmy had settled back beside me, hiding his face behind my arm.

A mile down the road, the woman indicated a turnoff, then half a mile farther an immaculate two-story house she said belonged to her parents. We stopped only long enough to let our passengers out then turned the car around. But when we reached the highway, the MPs had arrived. "Either of you nurses?" they asked, and when I told them no, they said we'd have to go back. Carol began to argue, but I took one look at the highway and understood. There was no room for us on the road. In the time it had taken us to drop off the young mother, the highway had jammed with cars carrying soldiers and sailors back to their bases. In the other direction, ambulances and vehicles of every make rushed the wounded to the hospitals in town.

"What'll we do now?" Carol asked, and Timmy started to cry.

"I'm hungry, Mama."

"I was frying him eggs when ..."

"Let's go back to that lady's house," I said. "Maybe she can give him something to eat. If they have a radio, we can get news."

The lady's name was Keiko and her family welcomed us graciously, bowing often—too often it seemed to me. In their limited English, they offered green tea and rice balls to Carol and me, and chunks of mango and papaya to the children. I took nothing. I was thinking of Wayne and those burned-out hangars, wondering what exactly he'd been asked to do. I'd never bothered to learn much about military procedure, but I knew that fighters came in waves; at least ours did when they drilled. I wondered if the second wave of the attack had begun and if my husband was still moving planes when it did. If a plane had been hit, would it explode if you tried to move it? Could it collapse? I knew that even if our military managed to shoot down one of the enemy fighters, there would be no controlling where the plane would crash. And I knew that sometimes even our own fire was misdirected and our own men hurt. I knew all the things that could happen, and that's why I couldn't eat.

Wayne is careful, I told myself over and over, listing all the traits that made me fall in love with him. He's practical, level-headed, kind. He'll be fine. We'll be fine. But that night, as I lay awake on a futon Keiko had laid out on the living room floor, my stomach hurt so badly I wrapped my arms around myself. Every time I closed my eyes, I saw that pilot's face again, felt the ground shake, heard the baby cry. I tried to control myself, but each time I started to doze, I'd wake with my heart racing. I gave up trying to sleep and listened instead to the bursts of

communication coming from the shortwave radio:
a call for doctors to report here, a plea for volunteers
with guns to patrol the beaches there. I'd go rigid each
time the radio went off, wondering where and when
the Japanese would land, how long it would be before
they overtook the island. Would it be safer to be with
this Japanese family or somewhere else? If they took
prisoners, would they keep the men separate from
the women? Would there be any way to get word
to Wayne? The only thing I did not ask myself was
whether the Japanese would let our men live at all.

I'd met Wayne in the summer of 1940. In addition
to my work as principal, I was attending night school
for my master's degree. Worn out, I decided to take
a vacation. I couldn't find anyone who wanted to join
me, so I came alone to Hawaii with $500 in my bag.
I rented an apartment near the beach and took hula
lessons and flower arranging classes and went for long
hikes. And when I wasn't doing those things, I was
lying beside the ocean letting go of all the thoughts
that usually crowded my mind. In early August, one
of my new friends invited me to an evening meal with
her and her boyfriend. On the way to the restaurant,
we ran into his roommate, a handsome, broad-
shouldered staff sergeant named Wayne Pollack, who
ended up joining us. For the next two weeks, Wayne
and I spent every one of his spare moments together.
When I boarded the boat for home, I was wearing
his engagement ring. All the way back to California,

I tried to imagine what I'd tell my family, how I'd explain why I was walking away from everything and moving to Hawaii, a place none of them had seen except in the postcards I'd sent. I would tell them, I decided, that Wayne and Hawaii just felt right to me. There was no other way to explain it.

Within a few months I'd tied up the loose ends of my life and returned to Honolulu. Wayne met my boat, and we were married that day. A friend lent us his bungalow by the beach, and we spent a week by the water getting to know each other in new ways. In the past few months, we'd bought Buddy and done our best to turn our military housing into a home. We'd even started talking about children, debating where we should raise them when Wayne got out of the service. In those first months of marriage, we talked about everything, including how we'd contact each other if we became separated. We didn't mention war. Never that. But I gave Wayne my sister's phone number, and I memorized his parents' address.

Now, lying on the floor in this house that smelled like fried fish, I wished we'd planned a place to meet, had figured out a way to get word to each other here and now.

When the sun came up, I knew I had to leave. I had to move. I had to do something. I scrawled a note to Carol and left before the others awoke. I walked the last couple of miles into town and finally found an

open drugstore and enough coins in my change purse
to buy a pair of underpants and a toothbrush. The
cashier was Japanese. She gave me the wrong change,
and when I pointed it out, her hand shook as she
corrected herself. There was an elderly woman beside
her who might have been her mother. She watched
me as I gathered my things, and slowly it dawned on
me these women were scared. "I'm sorry," was all I
could think to say.

I headed straight to Stan's law office a few blocks
away. By now my feet were aching, and I felt faint
as I climbed the flight of stairs. I hadn't stopped to
consider what I would do if Stan wasn't there, but
he was, thank God. He was gathering important
documents to keep them from the Japanese. When I
saw our dear friend, I finally broke down and sobbed.
And Stan let me, offering his handkerchief and a
glass of water, rubbing my back as I pulled myself
together.

"Have you eaten?" he asked.

"Not since before yesterday."

"Come on, then. Let's get you home to Sylvia."

———————

Today is Wednesday. This morning we wives were
told we'd be allowed back on base long enough to
collect a change of clothing. I caught a ride in with a
friend. No matter where any of us goes now, we stop
to pick up soldiers and sailors and anyone walking to
offer them rides. Every home, every school, even the
whorehouses, are open to anyone in need of a place to

stay. Isolated from the rest of the world, we're looking out for each other.

The closer I got to the base, the harder I watched both sides of the road for a glimpse of Wayne. For three days, I'd wanted nothing more than to come home, but one look at the piles of debris littering the base, the strafe marks on the side of our apartment building, the cracked or shattered windows, was enough to tell me it wouldn't be my home for long. War had been declared. I knew eventually the women would be encouraged to leave for good. Most would probably be sent stateside as their husbands shipped out. Our tidy little apartment would soon be just another place I had lived for a short time, just another harbor of memories.

The first thing I noticed when I opened the door was the smell from the garbage. I made a quick turn of the apartment, looking for a note from Wayne or some sign that he'd been here in the past three days. I found nothing, but there was no time to brood. If I didn't hurry, the MPs would come to order me off the base. And there was much to do. Sometime during the last three days, the refrigerator had turned off, and the food inside had spoiled. In the sink, those dirty utensils had started to rust. "*Never again will I leave dirty dishes in the sink,*" I promised myself.

Neither Don nor Carol was in their apartment. I'd not heard from Carol since I left her with the Japanese family, and I'd hoped I'd find her here. It was far too quiet in the building without Timmy squealing in the yard or the baby crying next door,

without the bark of our dog out back, without the
sound I most wanted to hear, Wayne's footsteps
outside the door. I began to hum to fill the silence
as I fished a box from the closet and filled it with
canned food to take to Sylvia's. I'd been setting aside
provisions for several months under orders from the
military. How lightly I'd taken all those precautions,
those alerts, those drills. We all had. How could we
not have seen this coming?

As I was closing the box, I heard Wayne call my
name. When he burst through the door, I jumped
into his arms, kissing his forehead and cheeks and
then his lips, feeling, for the first time, the start of a
mustache, and realizing he'd been too busy even to
shave.

"Are you okay?" he asked, lowering me to the
ground.

"Yes, I'm fine. I'm staying with Stan and Sylvia." I
took in the dark circles under his eyes, the slouch in
his shoulders, the burn on his forearm. "Oh Wayne.
You look terrible."

"We haven't stopped for three days. You can't
imagine the destruction, Margie. Nearly all the ships
and planes destroyed. . . I don't see how we'll ever get
back on our feet."

"Sit down," I said. "Let me get you something to
eat."

"No, I can't stay. I'm not even supposed to be here,
but I heard the women were on base. . . I had to see
you." He took off his cap and laid it on the kitchen
table, sitting down and pulling me onto his lap. He

buried his face in my shoulder, and I held him tight, wishing I knew just what to say. But then he gently set me on my feet and went to the closet. He lifted a sheathed hunting knife off the top shelf. "Take this."

I stepped back. "I can't."

"Margie, you *have* to defend yourself. I can't be with you all the time." He thrust the knife at me, but still I wouldn't touch it. Finally, he went to the box and laid it inside, folding in the flaps resolutely. When he took me back in his arms, I could smell his sweat and the odor of gasoline, and I started to cry.

"I have to go," he said, picking up the box of food for me. He waited while I went upstairs and threw some clothes and my best jewelry into a bag. I locked the front door then followed him out back to the car. When I got closer, though, I noticed the bullet holes in the hood, the shattered windshield, and froze. "Good Lord," I said. "What happened?"

Wayne looked away. "I parked it near the runway, and when the second wave came in, a couple of guys tried to use it for cover . . . One died on the hood, the other inside the car. I cleaned it up the best I could. . . I'm sorry."

"I'm not," I said, grabbing his arm. "It could have been you, Wayne."

We stood there for a moment, my hand on his arm. But when I jumped at the sound of a plane engine, Wayne nudged me playfully. It was one of ours this time. I pushed him back. "Don't tease me," I said. "You have no idea how worried I've been."

He tucked the box under one arm and wrapped

the other around my waist. "I'm sorry, honey. I've just missed you, that's all."

I leaned into him, and we looked out across our torn-up lawn and Buddy's empty doghouse and out toward the harbor where the sunken battleships slept.

"Have you seen Buddy?" I asked.

"No. I've looked for him, but no sign."

"I should have tried harder to take him."

"It's not your fault, Margie. He'll get by." He opened the passenger door and slid the box inside and then my bag.

"Wayne . . . when can I come back?"

"In a few days, maybe. When the bomb shelters are built. But Margie, the school is gone. It took a direct hit—"

"I'll get another job."

"I'll be working night and day. You'll be alone."

"I don't care."

"They'll start evacuating families soon. We can't wait too long to get you back to California. If it gets too hard to leave the island, it'll be the rich who get off first. You should go now."

I'd been trying so hard not to cry. "I'll leave when they tell me I have to or when you ship out. No sooner!"

Wayne shook his head and pulled me close. "You can be so stubborn. All right then, I'll see you in a day or two."

He handed me into the car. The sun glanced off the broken windshield, etching a laced pattern across the leather seat. I rolled down the car window, and

Wayne leaned in.

"Did you know the men who died, Wayne?" It was hard not to imagine what he'd seen when he found our car.

"One."

I didn't ask if that man had a wife or children. I wasn't ready yet to know. Wayne would try to talk me into leaving again, I knew. But watching him slouch back toward what was left of his base, I knew he needed me, and if we spent our first Christmas in a bomb shelter, so be it. This was my war now too. There would be plenty of work, I told myself. Plenty of reasons for the army to let me stay. I had always been a hard worker and a quick learner. I would do whatever they asked of me, including leave when the time came.

But until then, I'd take every moment with Wayne I could get.

Freer Than I've Ever Been

Lucy

I only whistled cuz I was bored. Me and Josie leanin'
out the window of the barracks, two young colored
men walking by. We were on the second floor and I
didn't think they'd hear me, but one looked up, and
Josie and I bolted back to our bunks, holding our
sides. Hester said, "You girls are too fresh for your
own good," and we laughed some more.

"Come on, Lucy. I'm hungry," Josie said, so we told
Hester we were headin' over to the mess hall, if that
was okay with her. But when we jumped out that
door, there they were—tall, handsome boys in their
army uniforms. "Well, the WACs are lookin' *good*
today," the skinny one said.

"Was that you whistled at us?" the other one
asked. He was a sergeant with broad shoulders and
big arms, but he had an easy smile and I liked him.
Josie started to answer, but I gave her a nudge. A
woman's gotta keep her secrets.

"Where you girls headed?" the skinny one asked.
"Mess hall."
"Well, we'll come along then."

I put my hand against the sergeant's chest. "You know you can't eat with us 'cept on Sundays. The mess sergeant has to count you in."

He took my hand and held it for a moment, with just enough pressure to show he meant business and not enough to make me think I oughta worry. His hands were calloused, like the sharecropper's sons back in Richmond County.

"Come on, girl. We're hungry. Whyn't you go in there and get us a sandwich."

I stood there looking hard at him. My father once told me you could read a man's thoughts in his eyes. It was the only such thing he ever told me, so I've held it close and taught myself to look. This young man had a smile in his dark brown eyes and nothing else. Josie took my sleeve and pulled me into the mess hall, but I looked back over my shoulder at that big man, and heard his friend call him George.

"Hey, Nettie," I heard Josie say, "fix us up some sandwiches. There's a couple good-lookin' Joes outside say they hungry."

Nettie stole a look from the window and put her hands on her hips. "Y'all go and get yourselves caught up with men you know nothin' about. You're gonna get your brains beat out one of these days if you're not careful."

I put my arm around her and drew her toward the counter. "That's why we're takin' 'em some grub, Nettie. To get a feel for 'em. Now don't that seem wise?"

Nettie just grunted. She made up the sandwiches,

though, and I noticed she didn't skimp on the
mayonnaise like she sometimes does with us.
Now wouldn't that make some of our poor white
neighbors back home mad: Nettie here layin' the
mayonnaise on thick, and them doin' without, just
like I'd have been if I hadn't joined up.

We sweet-talked Nettie into makin' us a sandwich
to share, cuz you should never eat big in front of a
man you're tryin' to impress, and we stepped out onto
the lawn, and that's how those two boys, George and
Marlin, come to ask us to the movies tonight.

From the time I was a little girl, I saw how hard my
mother struggled just to keep us kids in shoes and I
said, this isn't my kind of life. I didn't know how I was
gonna get away from it, though. I really didn't. All the
boys had gone off to war, so wasn't no husbands to be
had. I wanted to go to normal school in Fayetteville
to become a teacher. I'd always admired my teachers.
They'd come up the hard way, like the rest of us, but
could sure make do in that cold, cramped classroom
of ours with those used-up books handed down from
the white kids. They were the reason I could add
sums in my head faster than anyone in my family, the
reason I kept my nose in a book and out of trouble.
Thought maybe I could make enough money to put
one of my little sisters through later, but Daddy said
no. He didn't have no money to be sending no girl off
to school.

My brother was callin' for me to come up North.

Lots of our folks had gone, but for some reason that didn't sound right to me neither. At the time, I was workin' for an old lady who paid me five dollars a week to cook, clean and do her laundry. One day she sent me off to the post office and I saw these two recruiters—pretty white girls in beautiful uniforms—and I was struck. And when I stopped to talk to them, they smiled at me like I was their equal. I listened to what they had to say and rushed back home to tell Mama and Grandma. They was bitterly against me joinin' up, though. Said all them women were in the service for prostitution, but I didn't believe it. Next thing Mama and Grandma knew, I had signed up and was off to Des Moines, Iowa, for basic training. I look around now and know they was so far from right about these girls. The whole country's wrong about us, but we're showin' 'em.

"Hey, Hester, loan me five dollars," I say.

"Lucy, whyn't you ever got money of your own?"

"Cuz she spends it fast as she gets it." Josie has a laugh like the trill of a songbird and it makes me giddy just to hear it.

I sit down on Hester's bed and lay my hand on her knee. She's our master sergeant but acts like a mother hen. "Now, Hester, ain't it always you tellin' me never to go out broke? I'm just followin' your good advice."

Hester throws my hand off and pulls her face into a pout, but she reaches into her blouse and takes out a five-dollar bill. "Keep this in your bra, and if those fellas start actin' funny, you girls call a cab and get yourselves home."

I stand and smooth my skirt over my back side. I'm wearing my good uniform, my tropical worsted jacket and skirt, chamois gloves, garrison cap and my civilian pumps. Uncle Sam even thought to outfit us with a nice brown handbag. "How do I look?"

"You fill it out good." Josie says.

I look to the others for approval. There's Olive from Maryland. She's a licensed beautician with smooth, light skin, and I never go out without her checking my hair. And Luella from D.C. She said she worked at the Pentagon for a time before she quit to join the service, but she won't say why, and we all wonder. There are the girls from Mississippi that came straight off the cotton farms like me, and Margaret, an uppity gal from Atlanta that comes from a family of doctors. There's Chloe, who ran away from her husband, and them two girls in the corner sittin' too close to each other. I look past them, and past Sally too. She was a college instructor up North before the war. I think on account of her education someone promised her something to get her to join up and whatever it was never materialized. She's disappointed and bitter, and I steer clear of her. And then my eyes land back on Josie, who's here for the same reason as me, to shake loose the tight reins of her mother. They may not be high society, and I may not like 'em all, but they're good women. They take the flack that Uncle Sam throws at 'em and hold their heads high. They aren't afraid of hard work cuz that's all they've ever known. For the first time in my life, my world is bigger than Richmond County, and

Mama may not say it, but I believe she's proud.

I know it's not ladylike, but I can't stop myself lookin'
at George. I look at him through my glass when I lift
my beer and out of the corner of my eye when I'm
supposed to be listenin' to one of Marlin's stories;
I look at him square on when he talks to me cuz I
want to see that smile in his eyes and the casual way
he moves his lips, like he's got nothin' but time. I like
to watch him when he laughs. He's not one of those
men who throw their heads back and let it all fly; he's
more the type to drop his chin toward his chest and
shake his head while a chuckle shakes his shoulders.
There's nothin' showy about this man, and I like that.
I really do.

   I can hear Hester telling me that I'm too young,
and I don't know men. She thinks because I lied
about my age to get into this army that I'm still a
child she can boss, but I'm twenty-one, and I've dated
enough fellas in my two years in the service to know a
thing or two, and that don't make me loose, just lucky.
There's not a soul alive wants to spend all their time
drillin', sloppin' chow in the mess hall, takin' orders.
It's not expected for the men to hold back when
they're off-duty, so why should we girls behave any
different? But that don't mean I just fell off the turnip
truck; I know enough to push away the new beer
Marlin just ordered for me, for example, but I'm not
ready to wind down yet, not by a long shot.

   The others are doin' what soldiers always do—

white, black, male, female, don't matter—they're gripin''bout the service. I'm more than happy to join in.

"The women who recruited me made it sound like the army was going to be a rosy, rosy thing," I say. "Them in their fancy uniforms. Not like the mismatched, drab, ill-fittin' pieces they gave us colored girls when we joined up."

"You said it," Josie says.

"You know, them recruiters didn't mention how we'd be fallin' out at four o'clock in the morning, drillin''til breakfast, scrubbin' the floor, makin' up the bed."

"When that colonel come by and run his white glove cross the top of your locker, girl it better be white when it come down," Josie says.

I thump the table. "Flip a quarter on your bed and it better bounce."

"Clothes better be hangin' every piece just so."

We laugh. "No, sir. Not what I expected."

"Well, then, why'd you join up?" George asks, and he's watching me so close my chest hurts cuz I can't get a breath deep enough to fill it.

"Well, there wasn't nothin' for me in Richmond County 'cept being a maid, maybe workin' in a laundry. That's all they'd let us do. All our men were off to war, and I was related to half of 'em anyway." He drops his chin and chuckles, and I reach for my beer again just to give my shaking hands something to do.

"Yeah, so now you can work in *Uncle Sam*'s mess halls or his bakeries, maybe clean *his* hospitals," Josie says.

"Don't forget the motor pool," George adds,
and we all laugh. We'd all joined up thinkin' things
would be different, but things never really are for
us, and we shoulda known that. Like right now
we're sittin' round the corner from the first diner we
tried out tonight, the one where the owner pushed
past his pretty blond waitress to stop us at the door
and tell us we weren't welcome. Even after all these
months, we still slip into thinkin' that things might
be different here Up North or Out West or whatever
you want to call Fort Lewis, Washington. We
thought our uniforms would make a difference, that
us all being in the same war together would matter
somehow. Damned if we didn't get ourselves fooled
again.

"No, sir. Not what I expected," I mumble into my
glass. "But it got me outta North Carolina. And when
the war's over, I'm gonna use the GI Bill. Get myself
an education."

George raises an eyebrow, and for a second I
think he's gonna be like the other men, gonna say
something stupid 'bout how a woman should be
home raisin' babies. I've got myself so convinced that
I raise a finger to his face to stop him talkin', but
he takes my hand and lowers it gently to the table
and just holds it there, and now I know I'm feeling
something I didn't feel with the other GIs.

My mama used to say if a man looks at you
when you're talkin', you got his full attention, but
she didn't tell me that don't happen often. Most of

the guys I been out with sit with their chairs pushed
back, one leg stuck out into the room, their sides to
me. I know they hear me talkin' cuz they grunt or
nod, sometimes laugh, but their eyes are not on me.
They're searchin' out buddies from the base, watchin'
for white soldiers who've given 'em trouble, keepin' an
eye out for officers. Their eyes are busy starin' down
old white farmers and young white businessmen,
checking out the teenage girls at the counter and
waitresses in their starched pink uniforms. But not
this man. This man's sittin' with his legs under the
table, his feet flat on the floor, his hand holdin' mine
and his eyes on me, and I'm realizing when this fella
ships out, I just might cry a bit more than usual.

––––––––––––––

Before Fort Lewis, I was stationed at Fort Huachuca,
Arizona. There were a couple of black divisions
there—the 93rd and then the 92nd Infantry
Divisions— and those men were gettin' trained to
head over to the Pacific and later to Europe. Troop
trains pulled out of Fort Huachuca loaded with some
of America's best young, strong, black men. A few
of them had my name and address in their pocket.
Many of them never came home.

There was a four-foot wall on the base made of
concrete, and we used to sit up on that wall and talk
to the young men. Our company commander told
us not to, that it wasn't ladylike, that we should bring
them on into the day room instead, but we'd still hang
out there on that wall. That's my best memory of Fort

Huachuca. Us girls sitting out there on those warm
Arizona nights, the moon shining pretty and bright,
and it was like a party out there, laughin' and talkin'
with the boys who were going off to war. I'm average
height, and I've got good skin and a nice waistline,
but I've never had anything special to make me stand
out. When I was sittin' on that wall, though, I *felt* like
I was somethin' special. We all did, and there was
no harm in that. We'd waited all our lives to feel that
way. And then one night the company commander
took her flashlight, and she walked that wall and said
nobody better run. She lined us up and confined
us to barracks and that stopped us hanging out on
the wall, but that's how I'll always think of Fort
Huachuca. That's how I'll always remember those
boys I wrote to who didn't come home.

And I'm thinkin' 'bout them today cuz the caliber
of colored men here in Fort Lewis isn't nearly so high.
Most of these fellas are with engineering groups.
They're trained to build bridges and roads, and they're
a bit rougher round the edges, and I've been more
careful since I come to Fort Lewis, but that George is
different. He asked me to accompany him to church
yesterday mornin', and that kinda surprised me. I
guess it speaks well for what kind of man he is, and
Hester says I deserve a gentleman. But he's no stick-
in-the-mud either. After church, he came back to
the barracks, and we shot pool in the day room, and
every time I came up to shoot, he made me laugh so
hard I scratched the ball. After he ate with me last
night, he asked could he call on me again. I know he's

shippin' out soon, and I oughta say no. A girl falls in love with a soldier who's shippin' out and she's bound to either get her heart broke or wind up married too young, and I don't want either. I got plans for my life. I almost told him no, but I didn't, or I should say I couldn't. I couldn't say no, and here I'd come to think this army life had made me stronger.

Truth is I haven't felt this unsteady since I first stood on that parade ground at basic training listening to some white officer lay down the law and wanting badly to go home. Now I'm not sure where home is anymore. Richmond County seems so far away, and the girl I was seems like an old friend I've lost touch with. But someday this war is gonna end and Uncle Sam is gonna send me home to North Carolina, back to Mama and Grandma and all those other folk who think they know what's best for me, and I'm wondering if maybe, just maybe, it'd be nice to have someone around who'd love me for who I am now, somebody like George.

So my mind is spinning now, and it's hot out here on the parade ground. They say it doesn't get hot on the Puget Sound, but it sure is today, and I'm hungry and tired from marchin' and I wanna sit down, but we're waitin' for the two white battalions to enter the mess hall first, and I hear myself say, "If we're in the same army, why do we have to wait? Aren't we just as hungry as them?" But I didn't realize how loud I said it till our sergeant turned and stared me down and said, "Because it's tradition for whites to enter first, that's why." And that was the end of the discussion.

That's where it always ends and it don't ever get easier
to swallow, but it made me realize something: what
we want and what we get are two different things in
this life. If George ships out and never comes back;
if the war ends and I marry that man, settle down to
a house full of kids; if I take that GI Bill and make
myself a teacher, it'll happen like it's gonna happen
and me sittin' here worrying won't change a thing.
He's a hard-workin' man, he treats me with respect,
and knowin' he's somewhere on this base right now
makes me feel a bit lighter, like a Sunday hymn. So
when our battalion finally starts to move, I raise my
eyes up over the camp lookin' east toward home, and
I let all that anger and worry go because they don't
belong to me any more than the future does. And I
don't wanna feel them anyhow, because the truth is
whatever happens when this war ends, here and now,
far from Richmond County, I'm freer than I've ever
been.

Three Thousand Men

Attie

"I don't mean to pressure you," Attie said, "but you can see I'm getting on in years. If I don't find a home for these portraits soon . . . well, no one wants to die with unfinished business. You can understand that, right?"

The associate professor of art, who looked like a student herself, said she certainly could understand. She mentioned something about a grandmother who had died recently and a great-aunt to whom she was close.

I'm sure the coffee's ready, Attie thought, glancing over at the kitchen, not eager to get up again so soon. Perhaps if she waited long enough, the girl would assume she'd forgotten and offer to get it herself.

"We get contacted all the time to take people's collections," the professor said, "but I must say these are quite unique, Mrs. Fallon."

"Call me Attie."

"That's an interesting name."

"It's a nickname. I've had it since childhood. Please be careful how you hold those books. They're not put together very well. I was hoping whoever took this collection would find a better way to display them."

"I had no idea there would be so many sketches," the girl said as she took in the piles of binders spilling from the dinette table to the chairs and onto the carpet of the tiny, second-floor apartment. Behind her, several more portraits hung in matching frames on the wall. "So many men. What an amazing experience you must have had."

Attie lowered her right foot to the floor, then used both hands to lift her left leg off the ottoman. She'd overdone it on her morning walk with her neighbor, Becky, who had teased her about not keeping up. But Becky was only eighty-two. *When she's over ninety, as I am, we'll see how fast she can walk.*

"I was saying it must have been an interesting experience sketching all these men," the girl said a little louder this time.

"I heard you, dear. I was just thinking about that. When you get to be my age, you start to feel like you might have said all this before. I don't like to repeat myself, so stop me if I do." If she was going to talk, Attie wanted that coffee after all. She scooted forward on the chair and pushed herself up. The associate professor followed her into the kitchen.

"I met admirals, generals, kitchen boys, adventurers. Good men, bad men, every kind you can name," Attie said. "There was nothing I didn't hear. These portraits were the only pictures some of those boys had of themselves. My pictures went all over the world. There might have been others who did what I did, but not on the scale I did. So, yes, you could say it was quite an experience."

"Can I help with that, Mrs. Fallon?"

"Get the saucers down, will you? And the sugar. It's by the stove."

Attie poured the coffee into two mugs. She missed the brim on one, ignoring the burn as the coffee spilled onto her fingers. She handed a cup to the girl. "Tell me your name again. I seem to remember Janet, is that right?"

"No, that's my boss, Dean Steinmark. You spoke to her on the phone a couple of times. I'm Denise Bradley."

"Well, then, Denise, come to the table and we'll talk. Don't forget the sugar."

"Do you mind if I tape this?"

Attie eyed the hand-sized tape recorder, its red light blinking. "I've been a bit hoarse lately. Got this cough that won't go away. . ."

"No problem," Denise said. "This is just for my benefit. Just to make sure I get everything right when I give my report to the dean."

"Okay, then. Where do I start?"

"Are you originally from Florida?"

"Will that make a difference for the college to take my collection?"

"I honestly don't know, Mrs. Fallon. I'm just doing this as a favor for the dean. This isn't my usual job. Maybe you should just tell me everything. I can sort it out later."

Attie heard herself sip her coffee too loudly. Her

grandfather used to do that. She and her sister had made fun of him, of all the "old-people" things he did. Her sister died twenty years ago. Attie would start there, with her family, because every artist is shaped by her childhood. An art professor should know that.

"I was born in Butte, Montana, in 1908. It was a great copper-mining town. The wildest, wickedest city in the world—or so we liked to say. My father was a well-known newspaper editor. My mother a beautiful woman, an ideal housewife. I had a younger brother and sister. We used to go on wonderful picnics in the mountains. You must see Montana someday, Denise. So beautiful." She motioned for Denise to pass her the sugar. The tape recorder clicked softly as its reels turned, and Attie spoke faster.

"So Butte was an interesting city, but a cold, hard place to live. Every winter we went to California to visit my grandmother. In 1915, I went to the World's Fair in San Francisco, and the thing that thrilled me most was a painting by John Singer Sargent. I was seven years old and crazy to be an artist." Attie wasn't sure if any of this was hitting the mark. The girl was polite but distant, like a lot of young women today. Too hard to read. She waited for Denise to say, "Go on."

"After high school, my mother tried to make a housewife out of me, but that was impossible. I thought maybe I could be a pianist, but I was terrible. No talent." Attie laughed, but the young woman was absorbed in the portrait books. "I finally graduated from Stanford with a degree in English literature. That was 1930, the Depression. There were no jobs, but I didn't really need one. My family was in society, you see? I was lucky. So I started studying art in L.A. and then in New York at the Art Students League. You've heard of it, I'm sure."

"Yes, of course."

Finally, a little light in her eyes. "Then one day I heard about Pearl Harbor. Shall I tell you about that or stick to the art stuff?"

"Let's stick to the art stuff for now."

Attie reached into her skirt pocket and took out a throat lozenge. As she peeled off the paper, she skipped ahead in her mind. Sometimes memories came to her in disjointed segments—especially when she'd first awake and think Armand was still lying beside her—but when she actually tried to remember something, she found it would only flow in a certain order. Often she had to think a memory through from beginning to end to recall the middle. "Well, my family dragged me back to L.A—"

"Why?"

"Because there was a war on, and I was a woman alone. Those were different times for women."

Denise tsked loudly, and Attie felt a twinge of irritation. It wasn't that bad. There was something comforting about being a woman back then, knowing you were looked out for, even if it sometimes meant going against your own wishes. But women today didn't want to be appreciated just for being women. Things were more complicated than that. Today's women seemed more impressed with personal accomplishments. So Attie added, "I got a job in L.A. doing publicity. I raised a *million* dollars for war bonds."

The girl barely nodded.

"So when exactly did you start doing these sketches?" Denise asked.

Stick to the questions, Attie thought. *You're losing her.* "I fell in with a group of Disney artists and illustrators who had started sketching soldiers in their hospital beds. Portraits had always been my passion. This was a way to share that. The boys would send them home, and I'd get letters of gratitude back from their families. That's why I decided to quit my job and work full-time on the portraits."

"Did you charge for them?"

"Good heavens, no. This was my war work. We all did what we could back then. This is what I could do."

"Was it hard to get the men to sit?"

"Most were lying in bed. What else could they do? You'd go up to one, and he'd be looking kind of sad, and you'd say, 'Would you like your picture done?' and he'd say yes." Attie could still see the rows of beds: the war-wounded men sitting up a bit straighter when she entered, hoping for a few moments of her attention; the rushed, dog-tired smiles of the nurses; the occasional doctor in a blood-stained coat who looked over her shoulder as she sketched. More than fifty years later, she could still see the tears in the men's eyes when she handed them their portraits, could still feel the warmth she felt toward those strangers. Attie saw the girl checking how much time was left on the tape.

Attie cleared her throat and started again. "I had a little board about ten by fourteen that I sketched on. Mostly I used charcoal or pencil. At first I gave the boys the originals, but then I started making copies and mailing them the originals later. That's what most of these are."

"I don't understand. How did you make copies back then?"

"We had a machine, like an early copier. I think they called them duplicator machines. I had to use a special two-ply ditto paper and the machine could copy from that."

"They look a little purplish."

"That was the ink. But you can still see them pretty well, don't you think? I mean, that technology is fifty years old now."

"Hmm," was all the girl said, and Attie flinched. Then, thankfully, Denise changed the subject. "Who's this man, here? He's quite handsome."

"Oh, yes. He was a correspondent for *Liberty Magazine*. Had four ships sunk under him. See that picture of those three men on the wall? I sketched them at Terminal Island. They were admirals who had just gotten back from the *Missouri*, from witnessing the Japanese signing of the document that ended the war."

"Do you remember all of them then?"

"Now, honey, do you think I could remember all

these men? Most of them were here today and gone
tomorrow. You saw them once or twice while you did
their picture and off they went. I do remember this
one, though. He reminded me of my brother—here,
around the eyes, and, here, at the hairline. See the
way his hair curls out and then back at his temple?
This boy's name was Tommy O'Reilly. He asked if
he could write to me. Usually I told the men I wasn't
much for writing letters, but looking into his eyes,
I couldn't say no. He sent me three letters from the
front, and then I didn't hear from him again. One day
I got a letter from his buddy saying he'd been killed in
action. He told me Tommy used to carry my sketch
with him everywhere. He must have thought I was
Tommy's girl. He said he sent the sketch to Tommy's
mother. I used to imagine what it was like for her
when she opened that letter and saw the sketch,
whether it brought her pain or comfort. I used to try
to remember his face, and hope I got his eyes right."

"Sounds like he was pretty special."

"They all were. It wasn't just about the paintings,
you know? It was about being there with them in
those sick-smelling hospital wards, listening to their
battle stories, hearing about the friends they'd lost,
the girls they worried wouldn't take them back. I was
surrounded by men all day, by their off-color jokes
and the way they chided each other about their fears
and the tears they tried to hide. When the doctors
and nurses cleaned their wounds, sometimes I held
their hands, and when I painted, I didn't look at their
amputated limbs; I looked into their eyes. That's

where the *spirit* resides, you know? In the eyes. And if a boy's spirit had dulled, I painted it back in. They saw that when they looked at these portraits. At least I could give them that."

The girl was staring at her now, not at the books.

Attie took a deep breath and pushed her cup aside. She sat back in her chair and shook her head. "Don't get me wrong, though. Truth be told, I was looking for the great love of my life, the one who had everything. Well, they all had *something*, but they didn't all have everything."

They both laughed, and for a moment sat in comfortable silence until Denise picked up another book.

Attie cleared her throat. "Now, that's a different set, there. After a time, I got to sketching at officers' clubs and USO dances. This one here was at the big club in Hollywood, the one started by Bette Davis. That was a real lively group. Lots of movie stars. I would set up a table with a lamp, and when they weren't dancing, they'd gather round to watch me sketch."

Denise stood the binder on its end to flip through it faster.

"Careful, now. If you're looking for the movie stars, you won't find any. I wasn't interested in them. That surprises you, huh? I had no use for the Hollywood set. They put their pants on one leg at a time like the rest of us; they just liked an audience when they did it. No, I was there for the boys."

Denise glanced at her watch. "Do you know how many pictures there are in all?"

"Over three thousand."

"Three thousand men! You were a war-time industry all on your own." *A genuine smile this time.* Attie felt her eyes water.

She wagged a finger at the tape recorder. "You'll need to turn that thing off now. I have to use the restroom. Help yourself to Fig Newtons. There might be a box of Girl Scout cookies in the pantry."

"Oh, no thanks, Mrs. Fallon."

"I'll be right back then."

In the bathroom, Attie opened the medicine cabinet and took out her pill holder. She shook three pills into her hand and swallowed them with water all at once. The nurse who stopped by every morning got them ready for her. Attie was never sure which were for blood pressure, which for her thyroid, which to keep her regular, which for her arthritis —she just took what was set out for that time of day. When she was younger, she'd sometimes catch a glimpse of herself in the mirror, her light-brown hair and hazel eyes, and think she saw her mother. Not anymore. The face that looked back now was too puffy, too wrinkled, too heavy to resemble anyone she'd known. She thought about all the artists who indulged in self-portraits and how she'd never wanted to paint herself. Ironically, now that her eyesight was failing, she finally found her own face new enough to have an interest in painting it. Attie washed her hands and opened the door without drying them.

Denise was in the sitting area looking at a picture of Armand.

"That was taken just before our wedding."

"Did you meet him in the war?"

"Before the war, actually. We met at the L.A. Olympics in 1932. We fell in love, but he had to go back to Chicago. We didn't see each other for years. He married someone else. After his wife died, he called me up. We got married in 1970. We were soul mates from the beginning; we just got separated. A lot of people did in those years."

Denise set the picture back on the table, shaking her head. "You have *so* many wonderful stories," she said. "But I have to go. I teach a class at one o'clock."

"You can take a book, if you're careful. Show it to your boss."

"I don't think I should yet."

"Then let me give you an article the newspaper wrote about me."

"The trouble is, Mrs. Fallon, these sketches are all copies, and not even great copies. I mean, it would be better if they were originals."

"A few *are* originals. Sometimes the boys would insist I keep the portraits for myself."

"It's like I said: we get asked by a lot of people to take their collections. I'm not saying we won't take these, but I can't promise anything. And if we do take them, I'm not sure we have much space to display them. I just don't want you to get your hopes up."

"I'm ninety-one years old. All I have is hope." Attie clutched Denise's wrist and held on tight. "I'm not asking you to take the landscapes I painted after the war. I'm not asking for recognition for myself.

But some of these boys never made it home. Do you
see? There should be a place where their families
can go to find these portraits. There should be a way
for people to see what we sacrificed in that war, a
whole generation of men lost. I didn't paint anything
else those four years. I put all my energy into this.
Four or five sketches a day, and then I'd have to stop.
Your eyes can only take so much. This was the most
important work of my life."

"I'll do the best I can, Mrs. Fallon. I'll call you next
week."

Attie showed the girl out. Across the hall, Becky
appeared behind her screen door. She raised her
hands in question. Attie shrugged, letting go of a long
sigh. She waved at Becky and went back inside.

She rinsed the coffee pot and the two mugs and
turned them over in the drainer to dry. As she closed
the portrait books and stacked them on the end of
the table, she thought of something her mother used
to say: "We make the things that matter, matter."
Well, Attie thought, *these sketches matter to me. They
mattered to those boys. Therefore, they do matter. Is
that the logic, Mother?* She went back to the chair in
the sitting area and sat down, arranging the pillows
behind her back. She straightened Armand's picture
on the round table that had once belonged in the
house in Butte. She took off her glasses and rubbed
her eyes. On the news that morning, she'd heard
about a new art gallery downtown. In a minute,
she'd call them, ask if they had any ideas about her
sketches. Maybe she could get Becky's granddaughter

to drive her down. An image crossed her mind of herself as a young girl rushing the net on a tennis court. *I should have sat still more often. Saved up some of that energy.* She stayed with the image for a moment, then reached for the phone that sat on the table beside Armand's picture.

"I'm sure that girl still thinks this is partly about legacy, and it is, but not mine—theirs, and that horrible war's," Attie said to the picture as she replaced her glasses. *And here's the part you didn't explain, Mother: how to make the things that matter, matter to someone else. That's one of life's big mysteries, isn't it? When I figure that one out, that's when I'll let go.*

When the Dust Settles

Jean

May 20, 1942, Auburn, Washington
Tomorrow we're being evacuated. Today we had to get immunizations. We passed Mr. Oakley on the sidewalk, and I heard him say, "Damn Japs are treated better than we are. Where are *our* shots?" That man has never been anything but civil to us before! I started to turn, but Auntie grabbed my arm and whispered, "Jean, keep your head down." As usual, she thinks showing submission is the only way to avoid trouble. Maybe she's right. How else could we have managed to fit in all these years? But just this once, I would've liked to say something.

Now I must decide what to pack. We're allowed only what we can carry, but no one has told me how to fit my whole life into two small suitcases. This morning we burned everything Oriental and some of our important papers. Our hunting rifle and camera were confiscated when the authorities searched the house. We lent our piano to one neighbor, our typewriter and china to another. Since we don't know where we're going or when we'll be back, it felt

as if we were giving them away. They all promised
to return our things when we come home, but we'll
see. These people were once our friends, even after
Pearl Harbor, even after the curfew was instituted
for us. Now they're reluctant to talk to us, even to say
good-bye. Funny they can't see that the war has not
changed us, but them.

We'll leave the furniture. There's no time to sell it.
We told the Filipino boys who work with us on Mr.
Hollister's farm that they can live in the house till we
get back. They act sorry for our bad fortune, but I
can see them chattering excitedly. They'll be moving
in the back door as we're heading out the front. One
elderly couple has perched on our back porch like
vultures, asking for anything we can give. I finally
handed them our canned goods. I know they don't
have much money, but I resented it just the same.

Brother says the government waited till May to
evacuate us because the produce was nearly ready for
harvest. They let us do the hard work first, and now
everyone must leave their crops, their horses, their
equipment. Brother doesn't say it with anger. We
know better than to show our anger, but we feel it
just the same.

I'd almost forgotten I had this journal. I've never
been much of a writer. I found it while going through
my things just now. It was a gift from my teacher
when I graduated from high school. Auntie says I
shouldn't take it, that it might be dangerous, but my
teacher once told us that writing frees the soul from
the walls we build around it. If that is so, I may need

this book where I'm going.

May 21, 1942, Auburn

We're on a train heading south, I think. They closed the curtains to keep us from seeing. These filthy cars were pulled straight from storage. My clothes are covered with soot. Auntie and Uncle are sleeping. Leaving was hard on them. Not since they left Japan have they had to move, and even then, they left nothing behind. They had nothing to leave.

My brother is burning with fever. I've draped my coat over him, but still he shivers. He's so pale, and his breath is ragged, and he mumbles in his sleep and reaches for my hand. A few days ago he went to help a woman whose husband had been hauled in for questioning because he belonged to a Japanese organization. Coming back, Brother got a flat on the highway and had to roll the tire over a mile to a garage. It was raining and cold, but because he was Japanese, the men at the garage wouldn't help him. So he rolled it back. By the time he found a ride home, he was already sick. We tried to take him to the hospital, but they refused him because we were to be evacuated in a few hours. I've always been the forgiving kind, but now I know some things can never be forgiven.

But there is no one to fix my anger on at the moment, and that's probably good. It's only us Japanese in this car. Mrs. Wilson sits in front of me with her two kids, tagged like her luggage. Her husband is white, so he did not have to evacuate.

He'll stay and protect their farm. She knows she is lucky, but all she can do is cry.

There is a Japanese monitor on each car to make sure everything is okay. Ours is Ken Miyake. He smiles at me every time he passes in the aisle, and I at him. It's a good thing my aunt is sleeping. He helped me lift my suitcase overhead, but my sewing machine I keep under my feet. Auntie did not make me leave it after all. I convinced her we may need clothes in the camp. I can give up a lot, but not my sewing, and not the silver pencils my father gave me, the ones I use to write this journal. If the army searches our bags, they'll probably take the pencils, along with my jewelry, but if I'd left them, they might have been stolen anyway.

I can't sleep because I wonder where they're taking us, because I'm worried about my brother, because I want to keep an eye on our belongings, because I hope Ken will walk by again. I'm not scared, though. We know the Constitution. We know this is wrong, but you can't go against the president's wishes. President Roosevelt says this is for our own protection, as well as the country's, and he must believe that. He wouldn't lie. He says we can show our loyalty to America by going along. We Japanese are very obedient. We follow the law, we never take government aid, we work hard to prove we're good citizens. We take pride in that. So if they ask us to show our loyalty, that is what we'll do. But we don't have to be happy about it.

June 3, 1942, Pinedale Assembly Center, near Fresno, California

Auntie's so afraid they'll think I'm some kind of spy that she won't let me write much about this camp. I'll say only that there are more of us here than I expected (Brother thinks around four thousand) and the camp is much larger than I thought it would be (row after row of barracks with several families packed into each unit) and much uglier than I'd hoped (not a single shade tree).

I've been busy trying to make these awful barracks feel like home. Our room is only about twenty feet by twenty feet, so there's not much to work with. First we found some discarded lumber they'd used to build the camp and patched the holes in the walls. Then my uncle and I made a table and chairs and a headboard for Auntie's bed. When she saw it, she smiled for the first time since we left home. We've hung blankets to make partitions for our family, but the sounds still carry. I've not yet learned to sleep through all the night coughs and snoring, but I am learning to whisper when I talk. Auntie insists on it. "I won't have the whole camp knowing our business," she says. In this place, though, I have a feeling they'll know it anyway.

Tomorrow I must think of something to make the straw mattresses more comfortable.

June 22, 1942, Pinedale Assembly Center

I'm worried about Auntie and Uncle. Auntie and I are both quiet people, but now she barely says a word.

We line up at mess hall at certain hours. There's no Japanese food except white rice, and that's hard on Uncle. He was a hearty eater at home, but not here. He misses meat, which we get only on "meat days," and says that army food isn't fit for pigs. My aunt is eating very little too. She says the heat makes her faint.

There's much sickness in the camp. I'm getting over pinkeye, myself, and one night I was so sick with dysentery and vomiting I thought I was dying. This girl Janet, from back home, found me curled up on the floor of the latrine and helped me to the infirmary. "You better quit your crying," she said. "Looks like tears are all that's left in you." It's a good thing she came along. I'm better now, though, while my poor brother is still in the infirmary. His fever turned to pneumonia soon after we got here, and he has not yet fully recovered. I sit with him as much as I can. He likes it when I read to him from books I borrow from Mr. Nagaki, who was a teacher before they brought him here. It takes all my effort to get Brother to eat, but he must get stronger. He must.

July 8, 1942, Pinedale Assembly Center

Today I watched the people who had visitors, white relatives or friends from the outside. They're forced to visit through the fence under the stare of the armed guards in the watchtowers, and seeing that makes me realize how much I hate being caged up. Still, I envied them their visits. Mr. Wilson has decided to sell his farm and move inland, to the

Unprohibited Area, which means a certain distance in from the Coast. Then he can send for his wife and kids. How fortunate that he is white. We Japanese couldn't own land even before the war. Even if my family had moved inland, what would we have done? Better to let my brother get well and hope this war ends quickly. They say Pinedale is only a temporary holding center. We'll be moving again soon.

Maybe the next place will be better.

July 25, 1942, Tule Lake, California

This camp is better, but not by much. The wind is so strong here it blew my umbrella apart, and the dust and sand strike against us. They fill our clothes and the rooms we live in. It's an awful feeling. I miss the cool, wet green of Washington.

Auntie is miserable in this new, sprawling camp; most of the older folks are. But now that I know we're staying here at Tule Lake, I don't intend to brood. When I'm challenged to do something, I do it. I've been that way since I was three, since my mother and brother and sisters went back to Japan and left me with my childless aunt and uncle. For a while, whenever I saw a family I thought I recognized, I'd think it was my own family coming back to get me. I'd set up such a wail. But soon I learned to adapt, to think of my aunt and uncle as my parents. And when my brother grew older and came back from Japan, I was so happy. I had my family back again. I've always believed things work out in the long run. My brother likes that best about me, my optimism. And

Mr. Hollister used to call me his "resourceful one." So I know I'll survive this place if I can just keep away from those who want to bring me down. If I can just keep my hopes up.

August 2, 1942, Tule Lake

Tule Lake is built on a dry lake bed. Janet and I have been hunting for shells. We bleach them with Clorox and make them into brooches and flower clusters. Some of the Japanese have started selling them to the Caucasians, but I've kept mine to liven up our rooms. Today I gave them to Auntie. She's always admired pretty things. I've had no luck getting her to come to the baseball games or the talent shows with Uncle and me, but tonight there's a dance, and I thought if I could cheer her up with my gift, maybe I could get her to go. Maybe I'll see Ken Miyake there too.

August 19, 1942, Tule Lake

I passed Ken today as I made the long walk to my job at the diet center on the east side of camp. There are even more people living here than at Pinedale, which makes Tule Lake as big as a small town. I'm always looking for anyone I know. A simple smile is all I need to feel less lonesome in this place.

I asked Ken, "Where're you working?"

He said, "I'm a refrigeration man. Like before the war. I make nineteen dollars a month." He looked embarrassed after he said that. I think he was trying to impress me, and he did. I make only sixteen.

"Where do you live?" Ken asked, and I told him

Block 5001. I hope that means he'll come to call. He's a hard man to read. He said nothing when I told him my block number, just nodded and walked away. It certainly wasn't a romantic conversation, so why do I keep playing it back in my mind?

September 15, 1942, Tule Lake

Today I went on my first date with Ken. Auntie was glad. "He's from a good family," she said, as if that was all that mattered. It felt so comfortable walking next to Ken. He shortened his stride for me and took my elbow to direct me around potholes in the street or kids tossing balls. He looked straight ahead when he walked, like nothing going on around him concerned him. His confidence was reassuring, especially in this place, and it gave me a chance to study his profile. He has long, curled lashes—so unusual for a Japanese man—and a fine, broad nose. He kept a hint of a smile on his lips, or maybe that was just because he knew I was looking. He's twenty-seven, only two years older than me, but I feel like such a child when I'm with him.

We hiked to the top of Abalone Mountain on the north side of camp. Ken is as shy as I am. I don't think either of us said a word, but we sat at the top and watched the bustling camp. Thousands of us crowded into acres of flat, treeless land filled with long blocks of thirty barracks each, with clotheslines strung between them: shops, warehouses, administration buildings, industrial buildings, the hospital and on and on. A high barbed-wire fence surrounding it all. Ken pointed out the internees working in the vegetable fields outside the camp. I think he meant to suggest a memory of the fields back home, a reminder of our shared background. I didn't ask. Sometimes this place, this new life we've been forced to live, seems too big for words, and it was nice to sit quietly with someone who understood that. When he took my hand to help me down the hill, I noticed his palm was dry and his grip firm, and I responded by holding tight right back.

November 8, 1942, Tule Lake
I am more used to the camp now. Things aren't so bad here. I've arranged my life so there's never a dull moment because that's what brings people down. Ken and I go to movies or outdoor shows or dances. I take classes in sewing and crafts and languages whenever I'm not serving the ulcer and diabetes patients at the diet center. Ken moved out of the bachelor barracks and in with a family he knows, so he could be closer to me. He told me the other day that he checked into joining the army, but they told him no. His work here at the camp is too necessary. I was proud of him for asking and proud of him for being too important to let go.

When they took us from our home, I thought I'd lost everything, but the truth is, if I'd stayed in Auburn, I would've probably wound up married to some farmer, breaking my back for land that wouldn't even belong to us. Instead, in this hot, dusty camp, I found a handsome, ambitious man who looks forward, just as I do.

December 23, 1942, Tule Lake
Hard to believe it's almost Christmas already. We're going to a party tonight. I'm wearing a new wool suit I made from fabric I bought at the canteen. It took me months to save up for it. I've always taken pride in my appearance, and I look forward to wearing my new dress for Ken. Janet will do my hair. She's much better at fixing hair than I am. I've worn the pageboy style since before the war and have thought about changing it, but Ken likes it, so it will stay. Uncle tells me I'm like a schoolgirl with a crush and Auntie reminds me I'm not as young as I'm acting, but I don't care. I've never been in love before!

March 21, 1943 Tule Lake
I've been too distracted lately to write. Last night I slept in a chair by my brother's bed. He's been in the hospital again with pneumonia. Auntie begged me to come home last night, but I had this silly notion that if I left, Brother wouldn't make it through the night. I felt as if I had the power to make him stay in this world. Ever since he was stuck out in the cold that rainy night, I've had this fear he won't be with me much longer, that I'll lose him again.

They tell me there's no way I could really remember the day my family left me. I was only three, after all. But how could I forget? We were all dressed in our traveling clothes and ready to move back home to Japan. There was a tub of water in the middle of

the floor, and somehow I fell in. Auntie took me into
the bedroom to change, and when I came out, my
family was gone. Uncle was Father's oldest brother.
It was decided that one of the children must stay to
look after Uncle and Auntie. I'm not sure why I was
chosen, but I was. And for much of my childhood I
dreamed about my family coming back to me, and
then Brother did! He was fourteen, and I was nearly
twelve. It was one of the happiest days of my life, but
maybe our happiness wasn't meant to last.

I'll go back and check on him as soon as I help
Auntie with the wash.

April 15, 1943, *Tule Lake*

Brother's out of the hospital, but still quite weak,
and now there is trouble in the camp. The division
is growing between the Loyals and the Disloyals.
The Disloyals are the ones who answered "no" to
the two most important questions on the War
Department's loyalty questionnaire. Most of them are
from California. Many are *kibeis*, born in America,
but educated in Japan. And many of them are so mad
about our treatment they think we should turn our
backs on America for good. Some say we should all
go back to Japan. I think Uncle agrees with them a
bit. "I was born here, Uncle," I tell him over and over.
"I've never even been to Japan. America's my home."
But then I see the fence that keeps us in and wonder
if America will ever welcome us back.

A few days ago at mess hall, several Disloyals
stepped in front of Ken, crossed their arms and

seemed to dare him to pass. They said something in
Japanese that I didn't quite get, but Ken did. It made
his fists clench. Then they looked at me and said in
English, "A pretty girl like you should be with a man
who has honor." It was like when Mr. Oakley insulted
us outside the clinic. I knew what I *wanted* to say, but
I also knew better than to say it. Ken is so sensible
that he simply took my hand and led me back
through the mess hall.

It is the Disloyals who will be sorry for their
actions. The military police in camp keep their fingers
a little closer to the triggers lately. If we can steer clear
of the Disloyals, not get caught up in this mess, we
should be all right. But this ugliness between us is not
right. We're all in this camp together. Why turn on
each other now?

May 24, 1943, Tule Lake
Between Brother's health and the trouble in the camp,
Auntie and Uncle grow more sullen every day. We've
been waiting for a good time for Ken to ask their
permission to marry me. It's been hard to contain my
happiness. Auntie said today, "What makes you such
a songbird this morning?" I wanted to hug her and
tell her everything. Uncle says he thinks President
Roosevelt has forgotten us. "We've done everything
they've asked," he says, and he's right. We've followed
their rules, given our boys to die in the war, kept
the camp and ourselves clean and mostly peaceful,
pledged allegiance to the flag. Surely they can see
we're not the enemy. I want to tell Uncle we may

never get back what we've lost, but we can start anew
after the war, but he wouldn't listen. He's always been
a stubborn man. Maybe when Ken is my husband,
Uncle will listen to him.

June 20, 1943, Tule Lake
Yesterday I married Ken Miyake. It was a simple
ceremony in the barracks with only a handful of
people in attendance. Brother is ill again, so my heart
wasn't up to anything elaborate. The minister was
from back home. I wore a cream-colored suit I'd been
sewing for weeks, and Janet was my matron of honor.
Ken's best man was a friend from Auburn. He works
in maintenance and has access to a car he let us use.
We drove around inside the camp, and that was our
honeymoon. It was marvelous!

To be married is wonderful, although now, more
than ever, I wish for privacy, or at least thicker walls!
We have our own little apartment a block from my
family, but I will still spend as much time as I can
helping Auntie. This morning, though, I couldn't look
her in the eye. At one point, she just patted my hand.
I think I blushed ten shades of red. Once again, I'm
glad I have Janet to talk to.

Ken is as kind a man as my brother and when he
offers his arm to me when we walk, I feel like every
girl must wish she were me. Auntie's been very quiet
lately. In the year since we left home, she's become
a different person. She no longer has the heart for
change. But deep down, I think she approves of Ken
and me. If my brother were well, if the Disloyals

would stop making trouble for all of us, I could be truly happy.

August 12, 1943, Tule Lake

Things are getting more difficult now. The War Department has declared Tule Lake a segregation camp and are shipping in thousands of Disloyals from the other detention centers. Some of the Disloyals have turned violent. They're beating the pro-American men, threatening the women. We're scared of them. The authorities have segregated the camp, putting the pro-Japanese into their own barracks to keep down the fighting, but things are not improving. I'm scared for Ken and for my brother, who is a block manager. If they beat Brother, I know he'll never recover. The doctors at the hospital think he may have TB.

I still walk to my job at the diet center three times a day to serve meals, but I try not to walk alone. I was thinking the other day of the Chinese who, after Pearl Harbor, wore signs around their necks saying things like, "I'm Chinese, not Japanese," and how that used to upset me. Now I wonder if we should be wearing a sign that reads, "I'm for America, not Japan." What if the government sends in troops to stop the violence? How will they know who to punish?

The Disloyals speak more often in Japanese. I can speak only what Janet calls over-the-fence Japanese. When I was a kid, my aunt and uncle tried sending me to Japanese lessons after school at the Buddhist

center. I learned a little of the language and how
to write a few characters in *katakana*, but mostly I
goofed off. I had no interest in Japanese things, so
after a year, Auntie told me I could quit. Perhaps she
thought it was better for me to be just American. My
Christian name is English because Mr. Hollister, who
owned the farm we worked, suggested it. But how
much good will any of that do me and my husband
if the government sends in troops? I wish it would all
just stop!

October 18, 1943, Tule Lake

We're packing to leave Tule Lake! I can't find one of
the three silver pencils my father gave me. There has
been bloodshed and the army has taken over with
machine guns and tanks. The Disloyals will stay
here. The rest of us are moving out. Should I take the
muslin curtains I made, or will they not fit at the next
camp? I will have to leave the pillows I embroidered,
but I can make room for the sketches Brother made.
Wherever we're going, I hope it won't be as hot in the
summer. I worry about moving Auntie and Uncle
again, but I'm glad to be leaving. I'm tired of feeling
afraid.

I found the pencil! It had fallen under the bed. I
think I'll take the curtains.

October 26, 1943, Camp Amache, southeast Colorado

We were on the train three days. We stopped first at
Camp Minidoka in Idaho, and some were dropped

off there. Then Heart Mountain in Wyoming. Janet
and her husband were told to disembark there. I
cried and clung to her until Ken pulled me away. For
many years, I used to get letters from my sisters in
Japan. Then the war came, and the letters stopped. It
was like my family was taken from me all over again.
Then I found Janet, and she became like a sister. It's
been several days now and I still cry when I think of
her.

But I have Ken and my family and I'm trying not
to be sad. The train brought the rest of us to Amache.
It's a smaller camp than Tule Lake. There are thirty
blocks of twelve barracks each. Our block is in the
southwest corner. Ken will work in refrigeration,
of course. They tell me I'm to work as a file clerk
in the warehouse. I was never a good student, but
I guess I can manage the paperwork. I was ready
for something new anyway. I'm anxious to find out
what classes the members of this camp are teaching.
Tomorrow I'll get to work sewing curtains to fit these
windows to make this place more livable.

November 17, 1943, Camp Amache
It's cold here now and Auntie stays inside most of the
day. We take turns stoking and cleaning the potbelly
stove, a mess I could do without. I don't care for cold
any more than I do heat, but at least the snow keeps
the dust down. I'd hoped we would escape the dust
when we left California, but it clings to every camp.
I'm glad to be away from the trouble, though.

May 1, 1944, Camp Amache
It's springtime already. I've neglected this journal
because I spend so much time now writing to
Janet, who is busy with her new baby. How I wish
I could see him. Not until she left did I realize how
important it is to have a friend to share your thoughts
with. To be newly married, to be hoping for children,
to be ready to start a life of my own, but still to be
trapped in this camp is difficult. But talking to Janet,
even in letters, helps.

Outside the fences, on the shortgrass prairie,
wildflowers bloom in scarlets, blues and whites, and
the sight of them makes me long for a garden again.
But my nose is always plugged, and my eyes are
puffy. Not until I came to Colorado did I have these
troubles. The springtime has been pleasant here,
though. Each day holds tiny new surprises, like today
when I came back from mess hall to find a sand turtle
sunning himself in our doorway. We're far enough
inland now not to be thought of as a threat, so we're
sometimes allowed day passes to visit the small town
of Holly or even to picnic by the Arkansas River.
The taste of freedom is a welcome treat, but not
something I dwell on. I've always been a homebody
and, for now, Amache is home. Besides, my aunt does
not like to leave the camp. She feels vulnerable out
there among the Caucasians, who call us Japs and
watch our every move, who let their children stick
their tongues out at us. A Japanese parent would
never tolerate such behavior! When this war is over,
they'll want us back picking strawberries in their

fields or sacking onions, and if we need the money, we'll go. There's no point holding grudges. Besides, a little hard work will be good for our children.

June 10, 1944, Camp Amache
"When will your kiddies come, Jean?" Auntie bothers me constantly. I tell her when they're ready. I hope I'm out of this camp before my children are born. At times, that still seems possible. The war is turning in America's favor. Some of the men are leaving camp if they can get sponsored by someone on the outside who'll give them a job. Ken has talked about writing to friends in Chicago and other places to see if anyone can sponsor him. I haven't told him, but I almost hope no one answers. I can't stand the thought of him leaving. Not now.

July 14, 1944, Camp Amache
Ken has written to his friends. I've not yet told him about the baby, though I'm far enough past my monthly that I'm sure of it now. Leaving the camp and getting a job has become important to Ken, and I don't want to hold him back. I wrote Janet to tell her about the baby, and I think Auntie suspects. I have to sit down a lot in the morning or I feel sick, so now she holds my arm when we walk to mess hall for breakfast.

Yesterday Brother caught me crying. I told him I didn't want Ken to go. What if something happens to him out there? The war isn't over yet. Many of the Caucasians still hate us. I told him about the baby but made him promise not to tell. "Ken will be fine, Jean," he said. "You have your own family now. You don't have to worry about being alone anymore." He always knows exactly what to say to me. I know the doctors at Tule Lake were right, that Brother has TB, but he seems better here in Colorado, and sometimes I can imagine this place will cure him. That we'll grow old together.

August 17, 1944, Camp Amache

I catch a ride to the warehouse on a truck each morning, but the bumpy ride scares me. I raise myself up on my hands to try to keep from jostling the baby. I've never been one to pray much, but I pray now. I pray for a healthy birth and a healthy baby. Our care in Amache is okay, but it will not be the same as a real hospital birth. I admit I'm a little afraid. When I wrote Janet, I asked her to tell me exactly how bad the pain will be. Maybe I don't want to know.

I have a feeling it's a boy.

October 30, 1944, Camp Amache

Some people that Ken worked for in Auburn are setting up a business in Ontario, Oregon, and have sent for Ken. He leaves soon, but I will stay until the baby is born. Whenever the baby hears Ken's voice, he kicks. I should be excited about the life that awaits us outside the camp, but mostly I try hard not to cry. Ken has promised to come back when it's time for the baby to be born. I know he's a man of his word.

Maybe I'm just too worried because of what

happened to one of our neighbors here in camp. Her baby girl died a couple of weeks ago. The doctor here thinks she had chickenpox, but he's not sure. My neighbor goes on that if she'd been able to take the baby to a hospital, a *real* hospital, she might have lived. My heart breaks for her, but I can't let myself think about it. When I do, I feel like I'm bringing bad luck on my own child. It's superstitious, I know, but I can't help it.

I must stop by the school tomorrow and look at a map of Oregon. I'd like to know where Ontario is.

March 12, 1945, Camp Amache

Our son was born two days ago and I'm still in bed and only now able to write. There was no trouble with the birth, but it was a long labor. More than a day. Ken was with me much of that time. The nurses said they've never seen a husband so calm. I think that's why our baby is so quiet. He mostly sleeps, and I mostly stroke his tiny fingers and think how beautiful he is even with his pointy head. He has Ken's nose and my brother's high forehead. We named him Ronald. When Ken walks him around the room, humming quietly, it all seems so perfect.

Ken returns to Ontario tomorrow. I'll follow in a few months, when the baby is old enough to travel. When I'm not holding him, Auntie is, or Brother, sometimes even Uncle. The child is spoiled already, but at least it keeps him from crying and bothering everyone else in the barracks. And I don't have the heart to take him from them when I know we'll be leaving soon. But to be honest, whenever someone else is holding him, my arms ache to get him back!

June 7, 1945, Camp Amache

Once again, I'm packing. Ronnie and I will be going to meet his daddy soon. My aunt fusses with Ronnie's blanket and tries not to look at me while I fold our clothes. We both stay quiet. There's nothing to say. My friends tell me I'm blessed to be getting out of here. I will not miss the lightning that strikes so close you'd swear it could rip off your shoes. I will not miss my hay fever or this tiny room and the drafts that come through the walls. I can say good-bye forever to the dust, but can I say good-bye to my family?

Ken told me Ontario is a fine place, but his eyes did not fully convince me. I've told Auntie and Uncle they must come to live with us when they get out, but Uncle is talking of going back to Hiroshima, especially if Japan wins the war. I tell him that won't happen, but he says I don't know the Japanese people. They'll never give up. I look at my son and hope he's wrong. I want my baby to know peace, as I did. I want him to know his great-aunt and -uncle.

Brother, though, has promised to come to Oregon. I *know* I should tell him to stay here in the Colorado air, that I'll be fine, but I pretend it's his decision and I can't sway him. Maybe I'm not as strong as I think I am. But I look at Auntie and Uncle and the others who've been torn up by these camps, who seem smaller now, and I know that's not true of me. Maybe I've chosen to see only what I wanted to see; maybe

I've never fully accepted we were prisoners here. All I knew was this was the life I'd been handed, and I could let it bring me down or rise up to meet it. I like to think I chose to meet it and found my reward in Ken and Janet and in the pride I've felt being the person I've always been, even inside these camps.

We've beaten Germany and now all our efforts will turn to the Pacific. It's only a matter of time till the Emperor surrenders. It'll be over soon. But until then, Ken is going to have to help get me caught up, teach me about rationing and all the other things that have changed since we left home. And I'm still a little afraid of the outside world. It's been three years since I last lived among the Caucasians. I asked Ken to tell me truthfully how the Japanese are treated in Ontario. "This time I want no surprises," I said. He says if you ignore the sign on the water tower that says "No Japs," and if you don't expect to be allowed to use the bathrooms in town or be served in every restaurant, then things will not seem so bad.

I can't wait for Ken to see how Ronnie has grown. Our baby will never remember Amache. He'll know only the life we make for him in Oregon. I'm looking forward to having a yard again, to cooking my own food, to bathing alone, to baking a cake, to deciding for myself what I want for dinner. If we work hard, we'll soon afford a telephone, maybe a car. Any good I can do, I'll do it. We'll prove to our neighbors we're hard workers who will ask nothing of them and, in time, the war and these camps and all that we've lost will be behind us.

Living on the Wind

Doris

"I'd never let a daughter of mine fly," the old woman said. "It's just not ladylike."

Doris turned over the blouse and underpants she was washing in the ladies' room sink at the train station in Enid, Oklahoma. She thrust them hard into the water. "Oh, I don't know, ma'am. I'm standing here doing laundry. Isn't that the same thing you'd have me doing at home?"

The woman pursed her lips and snatched up her handbag. "In my day, we spoke with respect. I can't say I like the direction you girls are taking today."

Doris thought of several ways she could respond, but she had been raised to respect her elders and hadn't changed so much in these war years that she didn't feel a twinge of guilt at the old lady's rebuke. She swallowed her comebacks and wrung out her blouse as the woman huffed away. It had been nearly two years since Doris had had a full day off, and she wasn't complaining, but it was easier to deal with her exhaustion when people just left her alone. Today, especially, her patience was worn. She'd just heard a rumor from the private who'd driven her to the train station that the government might be disbanding the Women Airforce Service Pilots, or WASPs, as they were known. "But that's only right with so many of our own pilots coming home from Europe," the boy had said, meaning male pilots. "It's them what should be flying the planes now, don't ya think?"

"I think whoever's qualified should fly them," she'd shouted over the rumble of the truck.

Doris shook out her clothes. With any luck, they'd be mostly dry before the train to Wichita boarded. From there she would catch a commercial flight back to Long Beach to pick up another plane, a never-ending cycle of ferrying fighters and bombers and everything else to places like Newark, Oakland, Dallas, Enid, and then finding her way back via trains, commercial airlines, military cargo planes or, if she had to, buses. For this she was paid $200 a month and fed mostly by Red Cross volunteers who greeted her bearing egg salad sandwiches and Coca-Cola on the flight line.

"Army fools," Doris hissed, wishing she'd had a copilot on this last trip, a fellow WASP with whom to share her anger. More than ever, she wished that person could be Evelyn. Evelyn Sharp had been one of the most experienced women pilots in the country, a 1930s barnstormer with nearly three thousand flying hours before she joined the war effort back in 1942. Evelyn had died nine months ago, in March, when the right engine of her P-38 quit during takeoff. What would Evelyn have said about the WASPs disbanding, Doris wondered, she who had given her life for her country and received not so much as a burial in return?

Doris repinned her ash-blond hair, which fell in curls just below her ears, and straightened her battle jacket and slacks. It was a long ride to Long Beach, and she planned to sleep the whole way. Not deep sleep, of course—not on a crowded, noisy train—but rest sufficient to allow her to report back to base looking alert enough to fly. She picked up her wet clothes and went back to the depot bench, where she'd left the rest of her belongings with a young mother and her two-year-old daughter. She draped the blouse over the back of the bench and laid the underpants discreetly in the corner, sitting down beside them to hide them from view. Ordinarily she would have washed those clothes in a less conspicuous place, like the nurses' station at the base, but there hadn't been time.

"What takes you to Wichita?" the young mother asked.

"I'm catching a flight to California."

"My stars. I'd be so afraid to fly. I don't even like riding in automobiles. But a train feels safer somehow, so big and powerful, you know?"

"Oh, an airplane can feel that way, too. If you respect it, it'll take good care of you." Doris had been the next girl to check out the P-38 after Evelyn crashed and had spent extra time reviewing its handling characteristics. Every time she'd flown that plane since, she'd held it in the highest regard.

"No, baby!" the mother shouted, chasing after her two-year-old, who had cornered an unhappy cat.

Doris leaned back against the bench, thinking about the money she'd sent Evelyn's mother to help pay for transporting the body home. Several of the girls had pitched in, of course. They'd do the same for Doris's parents if anything happened to her, but now Doris wondered if they'd sent enough. She should write to Evelyn's mother when she got a chance, see how she was making out.

When she closed her eyes, it wasn't Evelyn she thought of, or flying, but the 1936 Olympics, where she'd competed as a fifteen-year-old breaststroke swimmer. She remembered Hitler up in his stadium box and the German woman who'd asked Doris and the others to shield her from view while she refused to shout *Heil Hitler*. "I vill not salute that man," the woman explained, "but if police see me, they vill put me in jail." Doris had been thinking of that woman more often lately, wondering what happened to her. The Allies were closing in on Hitler, and the war in Europe finally had an end in sight. That woman had found her own way to fight back, and so had Doris. But now Doris's fight might be coming to an end.

"Train's here," the mother said, returning with her daughter in her arms.

Doris donned her blue poplin cap and gathered up her still-damp blouse and underpants, folding them into the pouch she used to carry them. She toed her parachute bag across the floor to reach her briefcase. Inside her belt, she tucked her .45 automatic. A middle-aged salesman in a two-piece suit offered to carry the heavy bag to her seat on the train. When he asked her what was in the bag and she said a parachute, he looked at her incredulously.

Hours later, Doris awoke feeling someone's eyes upon her. A red-headed boy sitting beside her was watching her closely while his mother dozed.

"That man said you're a flyer." He pointed to the salesman across the aisle.

"I am."

"My uncle Jim's a flyer. He's in the Pacific. He was shot down once."

"He's lucky he lived to tell about it."

"Have you been shot down?"

Doris laughed. "No, I'm a WASP. We're not allowed to fly overseas."

"But you got a gun."

Doris had wrapped the pistol in her jacket when she sat down but, evidently, not carefully enough. The muzzle now peeked out from between the folds.

"Well, that's just regulations," Doris said. "Most of the time it's shoved so deep into the cockpit of the plane it wouldn't do me any good, anyway."

The boy looked disappointed. To make up for it, she said, "When I was about your age, I saw Charles Lindbergh fly."

"Did you?"

"Uh huh. And when I was a bit older, Amelia Earhart signed my autograph book."

"Holy smokes."

"I always knew I wanted to fly."

"Me too," said the boy. "But I'm gonna be a farmer like my daddy."

"Well, that's important too."

The boy beamed, then asked to hold her gun. She told him no.

Three days later Doris was in the air again in a P-51 Mustang—not an easy fighter to fly, but a fast one—headed for Newark. She'd planned her route from Long Beach to Dallas, where she'd spend the night; then on to Atlanta, where she'd stay over again; and finally to Newark. When the weather was cooperating, she could make the flight in two days, but not this time. She'd only be in the air a few hours each day, but that was fine. Any day that included flying was a good day. She sat on her parachute and the small pouch in which she kept her spare blouse and underpants. They gave her a bit of height, and the cushion she put behind her back gave her the reach she sometimes needed for the pedals and controls. At five-foot four, she was shorter than most of the men these planes were designed for, but that had never stopped her from flying well. It was early December, 1944, and she wore a sweater under her flight jacket today, and her boots. Though she wouldn't feel cold flying across the South, once she turned north toward Newark, she'd need them.

Like most of the planes she flew, this one had

come straight from the factory, and one could only pray there were no defects. But Doris had been flying too long to bother with more than a rudimentary prayer. She'd never had a close call, only minor hiccups, usually mechanical problems that were fixed when she landed to refuel. Doris gave credit for that to the women who worked in the aircraft factories—many of whom were her neighbors—who turned out planes so finely tuned that accidents were rare. She counted on their competence every time she climbed into a plane. Still, a good pilot never got too cocky. Something could always go wrong. Look at Evelyn.

Sometimes it seemed to Doris that everything she'd done in her life had led up to this point. Her father had been a doctor and a sports trainer, and under his guidance she'd qualified for the Olympics. Because of him, she'd grown up fit and athletic, a characteristic the WASPs had found appealing and one of the reasons she'd gotten to ferry so many types of planes. Doris's mother had recognized her innate curiosity, and helped her use it to complete high school early and then graduate from the University of Southern California. During those Depression years, her parents had sacrificed much to get her an education and flight lessons. Unlike some WASPs, whose parents refused to acknowledge what their daughters did, Doris's parents had been her ardent supporters. Now she was dating a B-24 pilot who shared her deep love for flying and understood that the cramped cockpit of an airplane was where she felt most alive.

She tried not to think of this as her final flight with the WASPs, tried only to appreciate the views of the Texas farmland far below as she slipped in and out of the clouds. It had turned out the rumors were true. Though she'd heard the ferrying division had moved heaven and earth to keep the women, the bureaucrats in Washington had decided to let them go. Doris had two choices now. She could go back to teaching at civilian flight schools or marry Mitch and raise a family. At nearly twenty-four, it might be time to settle down, she told herself, but as she tipped her wings playfully, it seemed impossible to imagine a life without flying.

As the clouds gathered close around the bubble canopy, Doris gazed out over the long nose of the P-51, wishing it didn't cut so much into her forward visibility. She'd be landing in Dallas soon and would use the nurses' quarters to freshen up. With luck, she'd find her way into the officers' club that night for a decent meal. She thought of Mitch, and her gloved hand went to the gold necklace he'd given her yesterday to cheer her up. Their talk turned often to flying—the thing they had most in common—but last night, as they sat in her mother's parlor, Doris fought to hold back tears.

"It's not right, Mitch. You said yourself a lot of the vets don't want to bother with qualifying in the newer planes. Why on earth don't they just let us fly them?"

"I don't know, honey. Why does the army do anything?"

"I'm a good pilot."

"I know."

"I deserve to fly."

"I agree." He lifted her hand and kissed it.

The look in his eyes was so sincere, so tender, that Doris lowered her voice, but her words were still firm. "I'm not saying I haven't been lucky, Mitch, but that doesn't mean I've gotten everything I wanted. I didn't get a medal at the Olympics. I didn't get to study engineering in college because it wasn't open to women—"

"But you got to *fly*."

"Yes, I got to fly. I did it for myself first and then for my country. That's got to count for something."

Mitch leaned over and kissed her. "It counts for everything."

As the plane moved farther into the clouds, Doris hit the bad weather she'd been hoping to avoid and dropped her hand from the necklace back to the stick. She felt her body jostle against the lap belt in the turbulence and leaned forward a bit in her shoulder harnesses to check her controls, which blurred the more the plane shook. Evelyn wasn't the only WASP who'd died. There were at least thirty others. Doris hadn't known them all, of course. They'd been stationed at bases all over the country. She often wondered what they thought as their planes went down. Did they believe they could still pull out of it, that somehow they could regain control? Did they pray or cry or shut their eyes or go down with

a heroic grin? Doris never pictured her own death.
That would be bad luck, but it was impossible not
to think about the other women at times like this.
Evelyn, too, had been en route to Newark when she
crashed.

   The plane took a sharp drop, sending her stomach
rolling. She gripped the stick harder, riding the
familiar waves of the turbulence. Doris focused on
the controls and took the plane up, hoping to get
above the weather. If she died today, there would be
no medal sent home to her mother, but she wasn't
going to waste any more thought on that or any
of the other injustices dished out by the Army Air
Force. She knew what she was capable of, what she
deserved, and Mitch had confirmed that for her
last night. How could she not marry a man who
understood her so well?

   As she rode out the turbulence, she felt a sweaty
itch beneath her cap and laughed at how utterly
unglamorous she must look, remembering the
comments the old lady had made in the train station.
In truth, she sometimes felt less like a woman than
like part of the plane. As the air began to stabilize and
the rich, high whine of the Merlin engine returned
to normal, Doris relaxed her grip a little on the stick.
Maybe flying wasn't ladylike, she decided, but it
wasn't "manlike," either. And that was what she loved
most about it. It was flesh and machinery, brains
and raw power. And the plane didn't care if it was a
man or a woman flying it. Evelyn would have known
exactly what she meant by this and been happy for

her.

"WASPs or no WASPs, I'm going to keep on flying," she'd told Mitch.

"I know."

"Till I'm too old to climb into the cockpit."

"I know."

"I mean it, Mitch. I'm going to be a mother who flies."

"Wouldn't have you any other way."

The Sight of You

Irene

Irene half-walked, half-ran the last quarter-mile to the pier in her high-heeled pumps, her toes pressing hard into the tips of her shoes. The plane had been delayed and then traffic was backed up for miles near the docks, so she'd arrived late at the San Francisco port, and now her brother, Clay, was not where they'd planned to meet. Irene did two turns in a complete circle, shading her eyes from the bright, November sun. She saw soldiers and sailors, hundreds of them, from all branches of the service. Throughout the four years of war, Irene had become accustomed to the sight of men in uniform, but she had never seen so many laughing, jostling, whistling, now-worldly soldiers in one place. How on earth would she ever find her brother in this mess? And if she couldn't find Clay, how would she ever find John?

Clay had been checking with the Red Cross daily for weeks now, trying to discover when and where Irene's husband, John, would dock. The plan was for Clay to call Irene in Los Angeles when he got word, and she'd fly—for the first time in her life and with

more than a little trepidation—right up to Frisco.
The neighbor would keep Irene's two little girls until
Irene brought their daddy home for good. For weeks
now, Irene had imagined this moment, when she
would walk along the piers beside hulking Navy ships
crammed with war-weary men. She expected catcalls
from the sailors, almost hoped for a hug here and
there like the ones she'd experienced on V-J night,
when all of Los Angeles poured into the streets to
shake off four years of war and deprivation. Now, lost
among all these eager young men, she thought of the
girl she'd been so long ago. The clear-eyed brunette
who always had a date and never missed a dance.
That girl would have looked at all these handsome
men and wondered which one would spend the rest
of his life making her happy. Now she stood among
them as a mother and a wife who had not seen her
husband for four-and-a-half years, had not even
known for sure until a couple of months ago that he
was even alive. Now she looked at the passing sailors
not to flirt, but to see if war had dulled the sparks in
their eyes, to catch a glimpse of what she might find
when she looked at John.

It was early November, the best time of year in
San Francisco, and she wished she'd left her raincoat
at home. She strained to listen for her brother's voice
over the sounds of ship horns blasting, longshoremen
shouting, street vendors peddling, children crying.
People bumped her shoulder as they passed. Soldiers
thumped their duffle bags against her knees. The
second time someone knocked her handbag from

her grasp, she simply stared at it as if she expected it to jump back into her hand. What was the point of picking it up?

If she could have found the taxi that brought her, she might have gotten right back in it and gone to her brother's house to wait for him there. That's probably what she should have done to begin with. Why hadn't she asked Clay the name of the ship or where exactly it would dock? Why hadn't she gotten more information? She'd had a tendency all her life to let Clay take over and even now, even after she'd learned to stand on her own two feet, she'd fallen into that comfortable routine.

If it hadn't been for Clay, though, she never would have come to a place as exotic and untamed as California, never would have found work in the airplane factory or the magnetic inspection shop. She would have stayed in Boise feeling sorry for herself, letting Uncle Walter pay her way, yes, but rubbing her nose in it too. If she hadn't come to California, she wouldn't be the woman she was now, but that was part of what scared her. *What if John doesn't like who I've become?*

A Marine scraped her ankle with his shoe as he stepped backward to take a picture of a pretty blond with his uniform jacket draped across her shoulders. He turned to apologize, and Irene waved him off. She watched the couple slip into the crowd, the girl leaning into the sailor, his hand sliding down to her derrière. Irene shook her head. Such a public display would once have been frowned upon, but the war had changed that too. Still, they looked happy, that couple, so sure of their place in the world, so sure of each other. Would she and John ever look like that again?

To reassure herself, she focused on her favorite memory of her husband, the day they first met. She'd accompanied friends to their church for an evening service, and there was John, a carpenter by trade, an assistant pastor by calling. She'd tried to listen to his sermon, but there was a slight humming in her ears, a buzz of excitement. His eyes came to rest on her so often she finally had to look at her hands. And at the end of the service, when she filed past him at the church door, and he took her hand to thank her for coming, he held on just a few moments longer than necessary. That's when she knew he was the one. She smiled now, thinking how handsome he'd looked in the late evening light. How sure he was of himself and of God and of everything that lay before him. In those first happy years of marriage, she'd come to believe that God did have his hand on John, that he was a man blessed, and not until he left for Wake Island did Irene ever question John's decisions.

In early '41, in the little house on River Street they shared with her uncle, he told her about the contract jobs he'd seen advertised in the newspaper, how all the men in the neighborhood were talking about signing on and some already had. He told her he could make better money than he did in Boise and get bonuses to boot, that it was only a nine-month job, and after he finished they could buy their own house. With the extra money, he could afford to work less and spend more time at the church. She said no, of course, she with a toddler and a baby on the way. She couldn't stand the thought of living without him so long, of worrying about him out on that isolated island far off in the Pacific, of having a new baby with only Uncle Walter to help. And she thought it was settled, until one day at lunch, he simply laid down his fork, strode out of the kitchen, and didn't come back for hours. "I signed up," he said. "I couldn't eat another bite until I did. I *know* the Lord wants me to go."

Irene took the two-year-old into the bedroom and slammed the door. While she sobbed, the baby stroked her hair, then nuzzled her neck, and finally cried along with her. And that was that. John left for Wake on a beautiful May morning, and his image in the bus window, waving at his baby, was the last picture of him she had in her mind. On December 8, across the International Date Line, the Japanese bombed Wake Island. On the 23rd, they stormed the island and took the men to prison camps in China and Japan, and from then on, not even God could tell her where he was.

But she'd never stopped believing he was alive, not even when word got out that some of the men had died in the battle for Wake; not even when the Red Cross told her they had no access to many of those prison camps, no information on the survivors, and no way to deliver the packages or letters she tried to send; not even when the newspapers started reporting rumors of Japanese mistreatment of prisoners, of torture, slave labor, starvation and exposure to the elements; not even when her own friends half-suggested she should get on with her life.

Irene had always believed God had his hand on John, that if He took him to Wake for a reason, He'd keep him alive. And He did. The proof of that came a month before the end of the war, when she finally got a battered postcard from John telling her he was all right. The words were stilted and most likely dictated to him by his captors, so it was his unique signature she focused on instead. She about wore that postcard out trying to determine from the slant of his writing the state of his health and mind. She'd slept with it on her nightstand these past few weeks, staring at that signature every night before going to sleep, waiting for that call from Clay. And now here she stood, still waiting. Always waiting.

Her hand shot out and landed on the arm of a passing longshoreman. "Do you know where I can find the ship from Guam? My husband was a prisoner and they took him there to get him well before sending him home. It's supposed to dock today."

The man took his cap off and scratched his scalp. "Lady, navy ships are supposed to do a lot of things. Could've got held up by weather or rerouted to pick up more men or held over in Guam for some reason or other. If it ain't here today, it'll be here tomorrow." He pushed his cap back on his head and moved on.

"But I don't *know* that it's not here," she shouted to his back. "I'm not sure where to look." He didn't

hear her, of course, just kept walking. *Tomorrow!*
she thought, angry tears burning. If she could only
take off these tight shoes, loosen her dress belt, let
go of the handbag that dragged at her fingers . . .
She looked around for a place to sit but saw nothing
through the wall of people. She felt a sob rising but
forced it down. She would not do this, would not
lose her composure now. She took off her raincoat,
folded it over her suitcase and patted the roll of hair
at the nape of her neck, then pulled at the finger curls
near her face. She checked for both clip-on earrings
and smoothed the front of the sapphire-blue dress
she'd chosen because it drew out the color in her
eyes. Finally, she straightened her hat, and when she'd
finished those feminine rituals, felt her confidence
return. This was how John would see her, strong
and able to bear whatever demons he brought home
with him, pretty and still young at thirty-one, with
only slightly broader hips and a few light crow's-feet
around her eyes. He'd greet a woman who couldn't
wait to take him back to a quiet life in Boise and bear
him more children, babies he could watch grow this
time.

She picked up her suitcase and began to walk,
stopping sailors and dock workers to ask after
John's ship, keeping an eye out for her brother or a
pay phone. She should call her neighbor and make
sure the girls were okay. Thinking of her children,
Irene checked again for the pictures in her bag,
photographs of Mary, who was nearing seven, and
Susie, who was four and a half, and pictures they had

colored for their dad. Those had been Susie's idea, she being the more excited of the two. Irene had done her best to keep John alive for the girls. For Susie, he was like an invisible friend. She'd talked to his picture every day, letting his stoic, Scandinavian face be both her guardian angel and her judge. But lately Mary was not sure what to think.

Since the war ended, Irene had started correcting the girls more often, especially Mary because she was older. She'd reminded the girls to watch their manners and keep their fingernails clean and sent Mary off to first grade each morning telling her to work hard so she could show Daddy what a smart little girl she was. No wonder poor little Mary seemed nervous about meeting her father. Irene had noticed worry in her daughter's eyes only days ago and quickly changed her approach, now talking nearly incessantly about how much John adored his daughter, how he used to play boats with her in the bathtub and take her out of the highchair to sit on his knee during dinner. And Mary's concern had turned to shyness whenever her father's name came up.

"Excuse me," a young woman asked. "Do you know where I can find a lunch counter? I've been here all morning and I'm starved."

"I'm sorry, I don't," Irene said. She remembered the apple she had in her coat pocket and considered sharing it with the girl, but then thought of John and how he might be hungry after his long trip. "But I'll walk with you," she offered instead. "I might find a pay phone nearby."

The girl seemed happy for the company. She told Irene she'd come today to bring papers for her fiancé, a warehouse clerk, to sign, and had waited hours for him to have a minute to spare. But there was no frustration in her voice, only excitement. "It's crazy, here, isn't it?" she said with a laugh.

Irene stopped.

"What's wrong?" the girl asked.

The salty breeze now blew at Irene's back. She felt she was going the wrong way, away from the ships, away from John, and she thought if she could just find him, she could feel what this girl seemed to feel, that the future was still full of promise. "I think I see my brother," Irene lied. "I've got to go."

The girl gave her a quick, happy nod and went her own way, leaving Irene facing the right direction but still completely unsure where to go. She set down her suitcase and sat on it, laying her handbag and raincoat across her lap. She leaned back against a wooden post and thought she could fall asleep right there. Her exhaustion didn't simply come from the recent sleepless nights anticipating John's return, but from years of feeling she had to sleep with one eye open, watching the girls after her night shift. It came from two years of four-hour round trip commutes to and from the Douglas Aircraft factory in Santa Monica, riding several buses and street cars to get there or carpooling with others, crawling along with no headlights in accordance with the blackout, tense with worry they'd hit the car in front of them. For two years she did a man's job, bucking rivets, working a sheet metal bender or a grinder, filing down parts by hand, lifting pieces that sometimes weighed much more than the twenty-five pound limit set for women. She gave her soul to that work to make sure the men who flew in those planes came home safely. Every woman at the factory shared that same determination while the lead men, who seemed to have no personal stake in the war, shot craps behind the layout table.

Like the soldiers returning home, she carried her own scars from the war, but she'd keep them to herself, never wanting to suggest that her own suffering compared to John's. What was a still-aching back or a smashed thumb or a burn on her arm compared to what he had been through? She made up her mind not to tell him about the run-down trailer park where she'd lived at first with hundreds of other families, all coping without men; about the ants that swarmed the kitchen and the stove that didn't work; about how you thought you were used to hardship until some small thing brought it all down on you hard, and you took your little girls on your lap and pulled them close and cried, "Where's your daddy?"

"I'm tired, Lord," Irene said aloud, standing to look across the docks one more time, her hand resting on the post. "Can't you please help me find Clay?"

In that moment, a movement caught her attention at the bottom of the ramp where a row of sailors and civilians were keeping to one side of a roped-off area near the water. There was Clay, waving, and she could hear his voice now over the sound of waves against the ships. Then the man next to him crawled under the rope and started toward her, and there was something in his walk she recognized and then something in his smile that warmed her and finally something in his eyes that caught her breath. His head was shaved, he was as skinny as a gangly teen, and his right arm hung stiffly at his side, but it was John. She wanted to rush to him, but her feet wouldn't move and her fingers held tight to the post. So she simply watched as he came back to her, as he'd promised to, and closed her eyes just as he put his arms around her, trusting her other senses to tell her this was really him.

"Irene," he whispered, his tears wetting her neck.

"I'm here, John," she assured him, and when he held her tighter, she could feel the ribs beneath his oversized shirt and smell a new aftershave that seemed too sweet for him. But when they pulled apart, he was smiling, and soon they were laughing, touching each others' arms and faces. Then she took his hand and held it close to her heart, and he rested his forehead against hers.

"You know what I've been dreaming about for four years?" he asked.

Her chest tightened. "What?"

"Your apple-cinnamon pie. You still make it, don't you?"

Irene laughed, releasing the tears she'd been holding back. "Of course I do, John. The girls love it, too."

"The girls," John said, his voice filled with awe. He took her face in his hands, wiping her tears away with his thumbs, and they stood there like that for a moment while her brother gathered up her things and the sailors cast them glances as they passed. "Let not your heart be troubled," John quoted from the Bible. And this time when he smiled, she noticed he was missing a tooth, but it didn't matter because this was the John she remembered, his voice strong, his gaze steady, and whatever challenges the future held, she could handle them. If the war had taught her anything, she now realized, it was that God had had His hand on her too.

"Come on, John," she said, taking his arm. "Let's go home."

Where She Began

Louise

"Mr. Garen would like to see you in his office, Louise," Mildred said. Mildred was Mr. Garen's secretary, but also the girl Louise ate lunch with every day, and this was the first time she had spoken so formally since the day Louise was hired.

"Is it what I think it is?" Louise asked.

"I don't know, honey. I hope not."

Louise took a deep breath and rolled up the blueprint she'd been studying. She opened her top drawer and lifted out a candy dish filled with lemon drops. "My mouth's a bit dry," she said, offering the candy to Mildred.

"Now, don't go sayin' anything you're gonna regret, Louise."

"I won't if he doesn't."

Mildred shook her head, took the candy dish, and gave Louise a gentle push toward the stairs that led to the second-floor management offices of General Radio, a test equipment manufacturer. The clatter of her heels on the steps had never sounded so loud to Louise, nor had she ever noticed the way the echo

reverberated across the narrow landing halfway up.
It was a muggy Massachusetts afternoon in mid-
September, 1945. Throughout most of the war, she
had worked six days a week, with time and a half
on Saturdays. If she was right about why Mr. Garen
wanted to see her, there would be no time and a half
this Saturday.

From the top of the stairs, a narrow rug ran
down the center of the hallway Louise now walked.
Ordinarily, if any of the managers or engineers came
out of their offices, the women would step off the
rug onto the hardwood floor as a courtesy. Louise
squared her shoulders and hoped one of them would
choose this moment to emerge. Just see if she would
move *this* time.

Mr. Garen occupied the last office, with a window
overlooking Massachusetts Avenue and the nearby
bus stop where Louise would likely be waiting soon.
She thought about the park she'd pass on her walk
home and the young veterans she'd see there drinking
discreetly from paper bags while watching the grass
grow. Louise expected to see one of those young vets
in Mr. Garen's office now and, sure enough, there he
stood behind the large window in the door, wearing
his army uniform. When she knocked, it was the
soldier who opened the door for her, not Mr. Garen,
who remained seated behind his large, oak desk,
smoking his cigarette. The office windows were open
and an oscillating fan stirred the air, but Louise still
felt a bead of perspiration trickle down between her
breasts.

"Come in, Louise." Mr. Garen stubbed out his cigarette. She watched him twist it in the ashtray until not the slightest ember burned.

"Well, take a seat, missy," he said, indicating one of two low-back chairs across from his desk. "You too," he said to the soldier. "No need to stand at attention for me, son. You're not in the army anymore." Mr. Garen bestowed a smile, and the soldier's entire demeanor changed. His face relaxed and he exhaled audibly as he sat. He was square-jawed, with a fine head of dark hair, but Louise couldn't get a good look at his face, a loose thread at the bottom of his uniform jacket having claimed his full attention.

"Louise, meet Corporal Harold Stine. He used to be quite the well-mannered gentleman. Seems the army drummed that out of him. Harry, think maybe you could shake the lady's hand?"

Harold Stine chuckled and offered his hand, meeting her eye for only a second before his gaze fixed on a place somewhere beneath her chair. It really wasn't fair, she thought. The whole war had been for and about men like him. Now, in the one moment when she should have the right to say enough is enough, and feel vindicated saying it, his humble discomfort made even that impossible.

Louise turned toward Mr. Garen. Let's just get this over with, she started to say, but Mr. Garen spoke first.

"Harry worked for us before the war. Isn't that right, son? Then he joined up. Fought in the Pacific. Was on Guadalcanal, didn't you say, Harry?"

Harry did that drawn-out nod peculiar to men, and Mr. Garen nodded right along with him, as if he'd been there himself instead of sitting right behind that desk through the entire war. Louise crossed her legs, folded her hands around her knee and looked hard at Mr. Garen, who cleared his throat and went on.

"Harry was awarded the Silver Star, weren't you, son? Damn fine soldier."

"I'm sorry, did you say, fine *worker?*" Louise asked. "Because I thought you said 'fine soldier,' but that can't be, considering you never served with him."

She tried to will the smirk off her face, but it wouldn't budge. Her mother had always told her that expressive face of hers was going to get her into trouble, and Mr.Garen's glare threatened to confirm that.

"Don't get smart, Louise. What I'm trying to say is this fella's got a family. A wife and two boys. His oldest wears braces for his polio. Those boys were knee-high-to-a-grasshopper when their dad joined up. They're counting on him, you see?"

"See what?" Oh, yes, she certainly was going to make him say it.

"Dammit, Louise. You're a smart girl. That's why I hired you. You know where this is going."

Louise waited through his pause, one eyebrow raised.

Mr. Garen pushed back from his desk and folded his arms. "All right, missy, if that's how you want it. I'm giving Harry back his job. Your job. You can

gather up your things and I'll send your last paycheck
to your house. You did your job well, and I'll write
any reference you want, 'cause I know it's just you and
your mama and you gotta work. Course, maybe now
that you don't have to work such long hours, you can
find yourself a husband. Settle down. Have some
kids."

Louise showed Mr. Garen the side of her face,
looking off somewhere into the corner of the room
as if she were considering an offer that hadn't been
made.

Mr. Garen rolled his chair back in and propped his
elbows on the desk, his hands folded with the index
fingers pointing out at her. "Louise," he cautioned.
"Don't make this difficult."

Louise turned back toward him and smiled. Then
she startled Harold Stine by placing a hand on his
arm and leaning in close. "I hope you have a good
time of it, Mr. Stine," she said. "I'll leave the latest
set of blueprints on my desk. In the bottom drawer,
you'll find a shaving kit. I'm guessing it was yours. I've
left it there all these years. Oh, and when you turn in
your purchase orders, make sure you go over them
well with Trudie . . . I think maybe that girl was hired
for her looks." She glanced at Mr. Garen just long
enough to watch his lips purse, then rose and went to
the door.

"Now hold on, Louise." Garen drummed his
fingers on the desk. "Mildred's talking about marrying
that beau of hers. If you're willing, maybe you could
take her place when she leaves. You're not as good a

typist as she is, but I can make do."

Louise hadn't taken her hand from the doorknob and now found she couldn't decide between a dramatic exit—one in which she marched out, slamming the door behind her—or one in which she spoke her mind. She opted for the latter.

"Mr. Garen," she said. "You didn't send me to MIT to train so I could type up your letters, and I didn't sign on to be one of the only women in production engineering so I could make your coffee. I'm glad I helped the war effort, but it might surprise you and Mr. Stine and all those other Joes out there to know I haven't just been killing time waiting for Mr. Right. Now, if you'll excuse me, I've got a desk to clear out." And she strode out before he could respond.

She still hadn't seen the color of Harold Stine's eyes, but whatever color they were, they were watching her now as she strutted right down the center of that rug.

———————

Good exits are hard to follow. Louise knew that, but she couldn't help but feel let down as she sat beneath an elm in the park near her house. It's not going to be easy to find a new job, she told herself, not with all the returning vets and with the war industry winding down. Half the women she knew had worked at the munitions plants or on the bases, and the other half had joined the Red Cross or the Army Nurse Corps. They were all back home now, filling their days cleaning out closets and painting rooms and doing all those domestic chores there'd been no time for during the war. Somehow Louise had assumed she could avoid that fate. How could she have been so foolish?

Removing her shoes, she rubbed her feet, thinking about all the steps she'd taken to get where she was. Mr. Garen was right. She was a smart girl. Pretty, too, with reddish-blond hair and blue eyes, and her parents always thought she could do anything. They insisted she get a college education even though money was tight. Her father had wanted her to be a doctor, but her heart wasn't in it. So she got a liberal arts degree instead. Her parents assumed she would teach, but her heart wasn't in that either.

She graduated in '38, back when there were no jobs to be had unless you knew someone, which she did. A fellow from church got Louise a position as clerk for the Norfolk County Courthouse in her hometown of Dedham. It was decent money and good hours, but the work wasn't challenging, so when Louise heard about the job at General Radio Company in Cambridge, she eagerly signed on. The extra money helped too, since the absence of men had driven her sister and her mother's friend to move into the house with Louise and her mother.

General Radio was a small but highly respected operation. It made testing monitors for electrical equipment used in laboratories, aircraft and submarines—sensitive material and some of it top-secret. Louise had immediately felt the importance of her work. Management hadn't wanted to take on women to replace the men, of course. Mildred told her about the arguments the men had had early on behind Mr. Garen's closed door. Outwardly, though, they expressed only confidence in their new women workers and, in time, many of them even seemed to mean it.

During the evenings, Louise would draw the blackout curtains and listen to news reports. She'd follow the war by putting pins in a wall map to mark the progress of the Allied troops, feeling that somehow her little bit of work was helping them advance. She saved up much of the money she'd made—with war restrictions, there was nothing to spend it on anyway—and now, at thirty-one, had a nice little nest egg. So while Louise had no specific plans for the money she'd saved, she liked knowing it was there, and that it was hers.

"Louise? What're *you* doin' here?" It was Rosalee, Louise's next-door neighbor, a pretty blond all of eighteen years old whose constant smile seemed a bit too practiced.

"It seems I'm out of a job, my dear."

"Oh!" Rosalee dropped down on the grass beside her. "Well, you worked too much anyway. Now you can have a little fun."

Louise said nothing.

"You're still singing at the USO tonight, though, right?" Rosalee asked. "I mean, I'm bringing my new boyfriend just to hear you."

With all that had happened, Louise had completely forgotten about the concert. Her instinct was to jump up and hurry home to freshen up, but it had been so long since she'd sat still in the middle of the afternoon, and she was enjoying the tickle of the grass beneath her bare legs and the crisp rattle of the drying leaves in the elm. Just this once, she thought, I deserve to take things easy.

"Did you know I wanted to be an opera singer, Rosalee?" she said, looking up at those swaying leaves. "My voice teachers at the college said I had a lovely contralto."

"Why didn't you become one?"

"Oh, I couldn't have made a living doing that, especially with the Depression . . . It seems I have many talents bound to take me nowhere."

Rosalee shrugged. "It was just a job, Louise." She stood and brushed off her skirt. "So I'll see you tonight?"

"Yes, I'll be there. But boyfriend or not, Rosalee, don't request 'I'll Be Seeing You.' The war's over and I'm sick of that song."

Rosalee's smile faded. "You certainly are in a mood today."

Louise watched her flounce away, only half-sorry she'd been so rude. Rosalee was too young to understand how far women had come, too young to remember when things weren't this way. But Louise remembered. In 1920, when she was six years old and women had just been granted the vote, she accompanied her mother to register at the local schoolhouse. The streets were lined with people screaming insults, and not just men, but women. Louise's mother had marched right past them all,

holding tight to her daughter's hand. "Society has
set a place for women," her mother explained, "and it
doesn't like it when we step out of line. But, Louise, a
woman needs to know how to fend for herself or she's
going to be left in the lurch." So Louise set her sights
on being a "career girl," and now that's how everyone
saw her. Somehow she would have to hold onto that.

A week after Mr. Garen dismissed her, Louise
enrolled late in a few classes at the university. It
didn't take long, though, to realize she didn't belong
there anymore either. The boys from the European
war, which had ended back in the spring, were using
their GI Bills to get the educations they never could
have dreamed of before. But in Louise's opinion,
they hadn't been home long enough to settle back
into something as structured as classes. To her,
they seemed to be still reeling from their newfound
freedom, still overly dependent on chums their own
age, still busy running from their memories of war.
And it seemed to have been too long since they'd
been in the company of good women. The catcalls
and innuendos and roving hands were disconcerting
to Louise and the few women in her classes, and the
juvenile pranks, crude jokes, and drunken outbursts
proved too disruptive for the professors. After two
weeks, Louise quit the college and resigned herself to
reorganizing the pantry.

The Saturday after Thanksgiving, Louise and
her mother came home from Christmas shopping

and saw a man standing on the front porch, his
head tucked down between the upturned lapels
of his overcoat, breathing warm air into his hands.
"Who's that?" her mother asked, but Louise couldn't
guess. When she came up under the porch light,
she recognized him. He was no longer in uniform,
and his face was in the shadows, but he was most
definitely Harold Stine. And now the question was
how to introduce him. Should she say to her mother,
"Why, Ma, it's the nice fellow who stole my job," or
simply call him by his name? Because he stepped
forward to take the packages from her mother, she
chose the latter.

"Come in, Mr. Stine," she said as she turned her
key in the lock. He followed the ladies in, set the
packages down on the entry table and removed his
wet overshoes. He held them dripping from his
fingers as he looked around for the best place to put
them.

"Just set those by the door," Louise said, moving
around him to hang her coat in the front closet.

He stuffed his hands in his pockets and waited,
head down. It was really too amusing, she thought,
how hard it was sometimes to meet even the simplest
goal, like seeing the color of a man's eyes. She barely
managed to stifle a laugh.

"Is something funny?" Harold Stine asked, and
it was the first time she'd heard anything other than
nervousness in his voice.

"Not at all. Can I get you some tea? How about a
piece of pound cake?"

"No, thank you. I'm here with a message from Mr. Garen."

"Oh?" Louise said. "Is it the phone that's broken or his legs?"

Mr. Stine threw an exasperated look at Louise's mother, who cast a helpless look at Louise. Chagrined, Louise stepped back and, with a sweep of her arm, invited Mr. Stine into the parlor.

"Okay, now," she said, taking a chair. "I'll be good."

Harold Stine sank down onto the settee across from her. "Mr. Garen sent me to tell you he has an opening in our department. You wouldn't be reading blueprints anymore, but you'd still be involved in production, sort of. In fact, you'd be working for me." At that moment, he dropped the hat he'd been circling in his hands, and when he reached down to pick it up, so did Louise. She got to it first, and their heads came up together, and finally, she caught his eye. His eyes were dark brown, at least in the lamplight, soft and a little sad, and now that he'd finally found the nerve to meet her gaze, he held it.

"Working for you, huh? Making as much?"

He didn't answer, just pulled one ankle up across his knee and held it there, his neck going red under his collar, and Louise felt a strange affection for him. She hadn't forgotten what he'd done for his country. Hadn't forgotten those two sons he had back home or how sorry he'd looked when Mr. Garen took back her job. She'd never really blamed him anyway, she realized. In fact, she felt sorry for him. Like so many of them, he was just trying to pick up where he left off. It wasn't his fault that where he left off had been where she began.

"This may surprise you, Mr.Stine, but I've not exactly been in high demand these past few weeks. And to be honest, I miss the work. So you tell Mr. Garen I'll come back, but I want to get bonuses just like the men and a wage that reflects my education. Tell him I plan to retire from General Radio and collect my pension. Now, I know I can't retire until I'm at least fifty-five and that Mr. Garen thinks he'll never have to pay out because no woman will ever admit to being that age, but just wait and see if I don't."

Harold Stine chewed his bottom lip. It was just no fun teasing this man, Louise decided, and come Monday he'd be her boss, so instead of tossing his hat into his lap as she'd planned, she stood up and held it out to him. "Just tell him I'll come back," she said.

She walked Harold Stine to the door and waited while he pulled on his overshoes and coat. She opened the door for him, but he paused before leaving, his hat back in his hands. "Things have changed a little with the work, you know?" he said. "It's been four years. You wouldn't mind, would you, if I asked you a few questions when you come back?"

Louise bit her tongue, as her mother had taught her to do, as she'd done so well with all those college professors and music teachers and even her father, good man though he'd been. It was something, after all, to be asked. It was kind of like starting over again, that's true.

But as her mother always said, starting over is still a start.

A Different War

Kathryn, continued

Kathryn sits on the porch of her parents' home in Cincinnati drinking lemonade and watching the neighbor kids play tag across the front yards. The waning summer light chases shadows across their faces and bits of grass cling to their bare feet. For them, the war will never be anything but a distant memory. It's already a year behind them, which is forever in the mind of a child. For Kathryn, it has only just ended. Less than a month ago, she was standing in a rubble-strewn street in Mannheim, Germany, sneaking leftover doughnuts to ragamuffin children at the back door of the Red Cross Club.

When the neighbor kids stop to catch their breaths, Kathryn detects a new sound, faint but distinct. Her ears are still attuned to war, to the subtle noises that signal danger: the click of a gun's safety; the creak of wood before a wall comes down; the low growl of a half-starved dog. But this sound is old and familiar and belongs not to the war, but to the happy times that came before it. She leans forward, seeking out its source, and finds it in a young man next door taking a pair of hand shears to the hedge separating their two yards. With his floppy, wide-brimmed hat, he looks like an old man bent low over the hedge, and not until he rises does she recognize Jerry Moore, who had been in high school when she left. "Evening, Jerry," she calls. He waves the shears, and only then does she notice he's missing an arm.

The screen door rattles, and Kathryn's mother steps out on the porch, a copy of *LIFE* magazine under her arm.

"Mother, why didn't you tell me about Jerry?"

"Jerry who?" She follows Kathryn's gaze. "Oh, Jerry Moore. Didn't I?"

"No, you didn't."

"Well, he gets on fine, after all. Always was a pleasant boy. His brother died on Iwo Jima. Now, I *did* write you that."

"Toby," Kathryn says. "He used to cut our grass."

Her mother flips a couple of pages of *LIFE*, then closes the magazine and looks hard at her daughter. "Are you all right, Kathryn? You seem so far away these days."

Kathryn doesn't answer. She's listening to the crickets. In Europe, even the insects had gone quiet during the war, unsettled by the bombs that shook their earth. Here, their song resounds so strongly it nearly drowns out the drone of a passing car, the soft murmur of the radio in the living room, the heavy breathing of the old mutt who nudges his way under Kathryn's hand. Kathryn gives the dog a scratch behind the ears. "I'm fine," she says, bending to kiss her mother goodnight. In her bedroom, she removes a stack of stationery and a pen from her writing desk and starts a letter.

The last time she put pen to paper, she'd been sitting on a broken step outside the flat she shared with another Red Cross worker. She'd written in a tablet laid across her knee, and though it had been evening there too, the sounds of hammers and drills had ricocheted off the cracked walls of the German neighborhood, never ceasing. Across the street, stray dogs and small children played on a hill of crumbled stone and concrete. From an upstairs window came the muffled sobs of a young wife whose husband had died in the war. There was so much rebuilding to do. Not just structures, but lives, and Kathryn sometimes wondered how the people would find the strength when she herself felt so worn down.

Now, here in her childhood home, the neighbor kids have been called in for bed, and Jerry Moore has given up his trimming, and there is quiet at last.

Cincinnati, July 21, 1946

Dear Esther,

How's life in Phoenix? Hot, I'm sure. Here too. And muggy. I'd forgotten how muggy it gets. I was sorry to hear about your grandmother. I'm sure it was a great comfort to her to have you with her.

I'm home now too. In my old room, in fact. It hasn't changed a bit since I left two years ago. Sometimes it seems like nothing has changed. Sometimes it seems everything has. Can it really only have been two years?!

Es, do you remember after we jumped off into
Germany, and they took us to a clearing station for
the wounded and told us to comfort the patients? They
showed me to a German prisoner, sat me down by his
cot and said, "Make him feel better." So there I was—
knowing all of two words in German— and him looking
at me like he wished I was his mother. What was his
ailment? Do you recall? Or had he been shot? Probably
that. I can't remember. Isn't that funny? You'd think I
would. I spent the whole afternoon watching over him.

You know, I never did hate the Germans. I hated
what they stood for, how committed they were, but I
never did hate them.

It's different being home. I can't describe it yet. Maybe
I was there too long. Maybe I shouldn't have stayed for
the Occupation but left when the war ended, like you did.
But then you had to, right? I didn't. I guess I thought
there was still more I could do. Now I wonder.

Kathryn stops there, but she can't bring herself to
turn on the lamp. She isn't ready yet for the memories
to fade. She needs to stay back in Europe, in that
place that has become familiar, rather than here,
where what once was so familiar now seems unreal.
In the dark, she changes into her bedclothes and lays
her head on a new feather pillow.

Two days later, Kathryn's mother invites friends
for tea, partly perhaps to cheer up Kathryn. Kathryn
has known most of these women all her life. She
went to school with their children and dated a few of
their sons. Many of these ladies had written to her

in Europe, keeping her up on local gossip and the comings and goings of old friends. How she'd craved those letters, each smelling faintly of the woman who wrote it. When she arrived home, they all came to see her, bringing casseroles and sweet rolls and telling her how good it was to have her back, how fine she looked in her Red Cross uniform—but also how she ought to do something with her hair and how she should stay out of the sun now. At the time, she'd found their concerns ironic, even funny. But today, as she carries out the tray of cakes and cookies, she winces when the conversation turns to wartime.

Oh we couldn't have made desserts like this during the war, the women chime. *No, not without butter. And that oleo never did taste the same. I got so sick of molasses in my coffee.*

When Mrs. Gilliland says, "Oh, yes, the best thing about the war ending was getting sugar back into my tea," Kathryn excuses herself to her room. She paces off her frustration, then goes to her desk and resumes her letter.

You should hear them, Es! Going on about rationing like cooking without sugar could possibly compare to what was suffered in Europe. How dare they complain to someone who's seen combat about how hard it was to do without butter? No one here has any notion what the war was really like.

Oh, I know, I'm the one who told you not to expect them to understand. I was always good at summing things up, wasn't I? In fact, I think we were

in the mountains outside Tirol when we had this very
conversation. Germany had surrendered only a couple of
days before, and we were listening to a radio broadcast
from the States. They said people were dancing in
the streets in New York, having ticker-tape parades,
celebrating! And there we sat with the men, listening
quietly. Not a person in that room felt like celebrating.
We just felt relief. That was when I realized it had been
a different war for the people back home than it had been
for us. But I didn't think it would bother me so much.

"I'm *trying* to move on," she explains to her father
when he sits her down the next morning after her
mother has gone out. She thinks of Jerry Moore and
his grass shears. Evidently *he's* taken again to simple
chores, while Kathryn still finds herself sitting in that
wicker chair every night, watching for the fine parade
of soldiers who promised to look her up. How can
she explain to her father—who has followed the same
routine at the shoe factory for years, who has never
fought a war or even left Ohio—how hard it is not
to have a situation driving her decisions anymore?
How she struggles to figure out whether she should
read the newspaper or sweep the floor, poach her eggs
or fry them, write to Esther or keep her thoughts to
herself. She pats his hand and tells him not to worry.
She'll be back to her old self soon.

Every night since she's been home, Kathryn's
mother has joined her on the porch, trying to draw
her into conversations about the church social or the

new twins born down the street. Kathryn had been close to her mother before the war, so one night she tries talking to her.

"Did I ever tell you about the club we had in Mannheim, Mother? We called it Rubble Haven. There was nothing left of that town but walls with holes where windows used to be. It was the displaced people that got to me, though. Carrying everything they owned on their heads and in their hands. No idea where they were going. When we'd reach those towns, they'd sometimes billet us women in the German houses that were still standing. Sometimes we'd go into those homes and their dinners were still on the table. They'd been ousted that quickly to make room for us. You can't imagine how that made us feel. So much destruction. So much despair, all because of the Nazis. I'll never forgive them for the things they made us do. Never!"

It is then she realizes her mother is crying. "My poor girl," she says. But that's not the response Kathryn had hoped for at all.

When she first came home, Kathryn marveled at everything—the clean sheets, the cold milk delivered each morning, the lights that turned on every time you turned the switch—and her mother had been right there with her, enjoying her enthusiasm, showing her how to work the new electric stove, taking her shopping for the latest styles. Kathryn had relished her mother's attention, had found herself walking arm-in-arm with her like old school chums. But after a few days, she realized those exchanges

were like the ones from her childhood, with her
mother acting as teacher and champion, not friend.
What Kathryn needs now is someone like Esther,
someone for whom the smell of Earl Grey tea brings
back damp winter nights in bombed-out London,
someone for whom the sound of sirens on a radio
program sends her dashing toward the cellar stairs.
She's heard neighbors criticizing some of the young
vets, the ones who spend their afternoons playing
pool or cards at the VFW, but Kathryn understands
their need to be together. She doesn't begrudge them
that, though she envies them. How nice it would be
to have somewhere to go when she feels out of place
in her own home, but the VFW is not for women,
not even her.

She hears the familiar *kshsht, kshsht* of the grass
shears and finds herself moving toward the sound.

"Evening, Jerry."

Jerry Moore straightens, his face registering pain.

"Where does it hurt?" Kathryn asks.

"Some days everywhere." He taps the clippers
lightly against his thigh. "I was walking behind a fella
who tripped a land mine. That's how I lost my arm.
Also caught a lot of shrapnel. Not sure they got all of
it. But I'm a damn sight better off than he is." He tries
to laugh, but when he glances at her, something seems
to tell him he doesn't need to.

"How long have you been back?" she asks.

"Little over a year," Jerry says. "I hear you were in
France too."

"For a while. Then Germany."

"Stayed for the Occupation, huh? That must have been something."

"Yes, it was."

Looking at the well-manicured hedge, Kathryn is visited by a string of disparate images: the smashed flower gardens and splintered trees of Europe; the cows that had starved to death in their pastures; child-soldiers lying frozen by the side of the road. Jerry Moore is lost in his own thoughts too, and maybe that's why it feels so comfortable standing beside him.

"Well, I'll let you get back to work. I just wanted to say hello."

"Nice to have you back, Miss Kathryn," he says.

For the first time in several days, Kathryn smiles.

You know what image I can't shake today, Es? The day the 44th Division shipped home and how hard it was to watch them go. Fifteen thousand men leaving, and the five of us girls still there. Remember how we felt so left behind, seeing them all ship out without us? Do you think they're okay? Our boys? The ones who made it home? Do you think they're coping?

The next night Kathryn makes a point to cross the yard and chat with Jerry. By the fourth night, she is waiting by her bedroom window for that particular sound, and when she hears it, she rushes downstairs to the kitchen and assembles a plate of cookies. She made them herself that afternoon, although after two years of not cooking, she needed her mother's help to remember how long to bake them. Now she walks them next door.

Jerry motions with the shears toward the porch steps and they sit, Kathryn with the cookies in her lap. How often has she played out this scene? The Red Cross worker and the lonely GI? But this time it's hard for Kathryn to start the conversation because this time it's not about making this boy feel closer to home, but about making her feel it.

"It's like I'm always waiting for something to happen," she says, "but nothing ever does. My father reads the paper each morning and heads off to work. Mother keeps the house up, boils potatoes for dinner, and I walk around with my hands behind my back. I keep turning around expecting to see someone from back in the war, keep thinking I hear planes coming in. Do you know what I mean?"

The boy says nothing at first. Then, "Look at that hedge. Does it look like it needs shaping to you?"

"No, it's perfect."

"Then why am I out here every night?" he asks. "Why can't I put these damn things away?" He throws the shears, and they watch them land points first in the grass. Kathryn pats Jerry's knee and stands.

"I'll take these cookies inside for you," she says.

"Don't go yet. Please."

She sets the plate on the porch ledge and looks down at Jerry, waiting.

"That fella who tripped the mine? He was my captain," he says. "He looked after me. When I close my eyes at night, I see him, or what was left of him.

When I'm out here, I don't see him. I just see the lawn, the flowers, that hedge."

Jerry starts to cry, and when Kathryn puts both hands on his shoulders to calm him, it is she who feels rooted. "It wasn't your fault," she says. "It could have easily been you who tripped that mine. But it wasn't, and there's no logic in it. Blame the war. Blame the Germans if you need to. Just don't blame yourself."

She sits down next to him again but leans in close, so he can feel her. If she closes her eyes, she can go back to a once-beautiful square now crumbling or a grey-brown field sprouting hastily dug graves. But this time she won't do that. She'll stay here, in the present. She lets Jerry cry but keeps her own eyes open, her gaze on the hose that snakes across the yard and the tabby cat licking drops from its nozzle.

I'm going back to the Red Cross, Es. Not overseas. I'm through with that. But maybe disaster relief. I've seen the kind of havoc man can wreak. Can what Mother Nature throws at us really be worse? I've meant to tell you that I'm happy for your engagement. Vernon sounds like a wonderful man. I don't think marriage is for me, though. I do better when I'm busy, when there's a bit of excitement in my days.

Please do send an invitation to your wedding. I'll come if I can. Sure it's a long drive to Phoenix, but it might be an adventure.

An adventure, Kathryn decides as she signs her name, is exactly what she needs.

Epilogue

The following is a list of the main characters in the order they appear in the book and a brief description of the real women on whom those characters were based:

Kathryn: *Dancing in Combat Boots*

Barbara Pathe has remained close to her Red Cross coworkers. They went through a war together. Though she held other jobs in her lifetime, Barbara remained active in the Red Cross, sometimes working on disaster relief—an experience she compared to war service except that the carnage was caused by nature, not man. "We were strong, we Red Cross women," Kathryn said in my interview with her, "but when I was overseas, I made the decision to be womanly because that's what the men wanted. They wanted someone who reminded them of the women they cared about back home."

Charlotte: *The Enemy You Know*

Along the side of U.S. Highway 34 near Greeley, Colorado, stand two stone pillars, the only remains of Prisoner of War Camp 202. But the camp was very much alive in the memories of Helen Schlagel Stansbury when I spoke to her. After the war, Helen raised a daughter and a son, then later worked as a secretary again. She died on January 17, 2001 at the age of seventy-eight. "There was something about being together during the war that drew us close," she said. "One person's sorrow was another person's sorrow. I would never want to live through it again, but I wouldn't take a million dollars for the experience."

Elena: Las Estrellas de Oro

The character of Elena is based on my great-aunt Lydia Treviño de Alonzo. A dark-haired beauty, Lydia had many suitors, but after the war, she married Joe Alonzo, the boyfriend who was waiting for her in the story. She raised two daughters and later returned to work after her husband died. "It was hard for a young lady to have such a high post," Lydia told me, "but back then people took you for how you behaved, and I was always called a lady—by the salesmen, by my customers, by my friends. I think it's been a plus to have that respect."

Marjorie: Black Smoke Rising

To most Americans in 1941, Pearl Harbor was an unknown place. To Dorothy Davidson Nabors, it was home. Born in Ontario, Canada, Dorothy graduated from Whittier College in California in 1935 and began teaching. She was an athletic twenty-seven-year-old when she married Bonnie Nabors in 1941. After the war, Dorothy raised one son then resumed her career in education. She passed away April 20, 2001 at the age of eighty-six. "Pearl Harbor changed your attitude toward life and toward people," Dorothy said. "It taught me how unimportant things are. What value are they? They can be gone just like that."

Lucy: Freer Than I've Ever Been

"The white battalions entered the mess hall first. One of our girls asked our sergeant why that was, and she said, 'Because it's tradition for white people to enter the building first.' No questions asked. No more discussion. That's just the way it was," recalled Judy Covington McKinnon. In the spring of 1942, Judy lied about her age to become one of the first women to enlist in the newly formed Women's Auxiliary Army Corps (WAAC), later the Women's Army Corps (WAC). She was a naive nineteen-year-old, "a little on the wild side, but careful, too—fairly nice lookin' with nice skin and a pretty good figure." She met her husband, Cornelius, in the army and married him in 1945. She later raised three children and, when I spoke to her, was selling home accessories.

Attie: Three Thousand Men

In hundreds of homes across the country may be displayed some of the three thousand sketches of servicemen drawn by Mildred "Dabney" Shearer Didot. Dabney was thirty-three years old in 1941, with hazel eyes and a romantic spirit. After the war, Dabney continued her life of high adventure, traveling extensively, marrying and divorcing the son of the Nicaraguan president, and later settling down with her soul mate. Her unique service to the war effort stemmed from her talent for and love of portraiture, a passion she pursued until her death on February 25, 2001, at age ninety-three. "I think the

war broadened women's points of view," Dabney told
me. "They found they could be individuals and do
what they wanted, whether they were married or not."

Doris: Living on the Wind

At five-foot four, Iris Cummings Critchell could
barely reach the controls of the airplanes she piloted
for the ferry command. After the war, Iris married
Howard, her B-24 pilot, and raised two children.
She also served on the board of directors for
Transcontinental Airways, prepared college courses
in aviation, and flew in Powder Puff Derbies. At age
eighty-six, Iris is still flying. "The status of women
wasn't too free back then," she admitted to me, "but
the airplane didn't care if it was a man or woman
flying it."

Jean: When the Dust Settles

Frances Itabashi Nishimura is a *nisei*, an American-
born offspring of Japanese immigrants. She was
one of 120,000 Japanese and Japanese-Americans
removed from the West Coast and interned in
relocation camps in 1942. Frances was twenty-six
when she married her husband, Shizuo, in the camp.
Later, while raising four children, she became active
in civic organizations in Ontario, Oregon, giving
back cheerfully to the country that had incarcerated
her for most of the war. Through it all, she never
stopped thinking of herself as an American citizen.
"I felt really dumb when I came out of the camp;
for example, I knew nothing about rationing. I had

to work hard to catch up to the outside world. But
I learned to avoid negative things. Whatever good
there was to be done, I did it."

Irene: The Sight of You
Clarine Riordan Johnson was twenty-seven and
pregnant when her husband, Oreal, left home
to work on Wake Island. When Oreal returned
from the prison camps, his world had changed.
Readjustment was hard for him and for Clarine,
who nursed him back to health, comforted him after
his nightmares, and helped him get acquainted with
his young daughters. Her patience paid off, though,
and they went on to have four more girls. "It was an
extremely tough life during the war if you had kids to
support," she said, "but the hardest part was just plain
missing Oreal."

Louise: Where She Began
In the 1940s, Helen Goring was tall and slim and
wore her reddish-blond hair in the popular pageboy
style. The first person in her family to attend college,
she graduated Boston University with a degree
in philosophy, but says that, at the time, she was
really "a frustrated opera singer." At the end of the
war she continued to work for General Radio for
twenty-three years. Then, fed up with the work
environment for women, she turned to a career
in teaching, obtaining two master's degrees and
eventually founding the anthropology department
at Hillsborough Community College in Tampa,

Florida. "Back then," Helen said, "we were second-class citizens. Yet somehow I'd gotten the lesson from my parents that a woman had to learn to fend for herself or she was going to be left in the lurch."

About the Author

Teresa R. Funke is the author of *Remember Wake*, an award-winning novel based on a true story from WWII. Her short stories and essays have appeared in numerous commercial and literary magazines and anthologies. Two of her essays have been listed as Notable Essays of 2002 and 2004 by the prestigious Best American Essays series.

Teresa has worked as a researcher for PBS and several museums. Her articles and columns have appeared in magazines and newspapers around the country. A popular speaker, presenter and writer's coach, Teresa is also the on-screen host of a writers' video series called The Write Series.

Teresa also enjoys writing for children. Her Home-Front Heroes series for middle-grade readers is fast becoming popular among young readers and teachers. Please check her website for more information about Teresa and her books, www.teresafunke.com.

Also by Teresa R. Funke

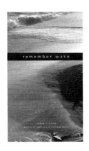

Remember Wake

A novel based on a true story

291 pages ✦ softcover
ISBN 978-1-935571-08-7

Available at amazon.com,
barnesandnoble.com and teresafunke.com.

December, 1941—While the world focuses on the
carnage at Pearl Harbor, tiny Wake Island 2,300
miles west is also under attack. On it are 1,200
civilians and a small detachment of marines. This
frightened, under-equipped band of Americans will
hold the mighty Japanese navy at bay for sixteen
days before succumbing to the sweeping invasion.
"Remember Wake" becomes a battle cry for a nation
marching to war.

Now prisoners of the Emperor, Colin Finnely and
the others are crowded aboard a notorious Japanese
hell-ship bound for Asia, where they will suffer four
long years as slave laborers in disease-infested camps.
They will die by the hundreds.

With only one reason to live—his love for his
fiancée, Maggie Braun—Colin struggles to survive
torture and inhuman conditions.

And on the home front, Maggie, unsure if Colin is
even alive, faces agonizing decisions that may alter
both their lives.

Reader comments for *Remember Wake*

"A book club must."
– A barnesandnoble.com reviewer

"*Remember Wake* is a compelling book filled with details of World War II at home and abroad. Promising young writer Teresa R. Funke tells a story of young lovers caught up in the events of wartime that will haunt you long after you've finished the book."
– Sandra Dallas, author of *Alice's Tulips* and
  The Persian Pickle Club

"Teresa Funke's novel *Remember Wake* is a great addition to your historical fiction collection. This is a rich re-telling of the WWII Battle of Wake Island. The novel brings to life an inspiring story of bravery, stoic suffering and love. A good read for historians and romantics alike."
– *Colorado Libraries Journal*

"The history behind *Remember Wake* is intriguing. A handful of Americans held off the Japanese navy for sixteen days at Wake Island, aided by the heroic efforts of armed civilians. The author's depictions of prison camps are authentic and harrowing.

The novel traces the effects of war on its two civilian protagonists, ordinary people caught in the tides of history. Maggie and Colin are heroic, not because they control their circumstances, but because they survive them. The story is always well told, and the scenes between Maggie and William Preston, a would-be suitor, are genuinely heartbreaking. *Remember Wake* is a great read."
– Brian Kaufman, author of *The Breach*

A wonderful and informative book

I couldn't put it down! This is such an inspiring story! The main characters went through such a terrible battle to survive the prison ships and prison camps. It's incredible that this is based on true facts! The author really shows you what it would be like to survive a war.

– Carla Wilkins, barnesandnoble.com reviewer

A great history book

Remember Wake did more for teaching history to my kids than their Social Studies textbooks did in a year because the novel interested them. I highly recommend it for all school libraries.

– Lorraine Nuxoll, barnesandnoble.com reviewer

Recalling an oft-forgotten story

Remember Wake (a real page-turner) had me fascinated from the first few pages. The characters were likeable and interesting, moreover, the images (especially those from the POW camps) were real and powerful.

– A reporter for the *Lewiston Morning Tribune*, amazon.com review

Fascinating read

A wonderful, interesting read about Wake Island and its role in WWII, brought to life through two fascinating characters. I particularly enjoyed learning about the hardships experience by women left at home. A terrific book!

– A reader from Fort Collins, amazon.com review

An excerpt from *Remember Wake*

Boise

They had gathered around Eddie's kitchen table ten minutes before noon on Monday morning, December 8th. A plate of sandwiches grew stale in front of them while the coffeepot percolated loudly. A small radio warbled a song about bluebirds over white cliffs, but they had not gathered to hear music. They'd come together to hear the President declare war.

Maggie concentrated on the wood grain in Eddie's dark pine table, tracing the lines with her finger as they swirled and stretched across the surface—anything to keep from meeting her mother's gaze. It was infuriating to see the way Agnes looked at her with pity and concern, as if she already knew Colin was dead. She'd been hovering over Maggie since they heard the news yesterday about Pearl Harbor, denying Maggie the time to herself she so desperately needed, forcing her to take walks and help with housework, thinking, as usual, she knew what Maggie needed—to keep busy, to keep her mind off what had happened.

Maggie thought of Colin's mother. She had wanted to be with Laura today, but Agnes had insisted she stay home with her own family. And she thought of Ellen and wondered if her hands were still, just this once.

But mostly she thought about Colin, of the letters she'd found in her uncle's car, the ones she'd asked him to mail a few weeks ago and he'd apparently forgotten. What must Colin have thought when he received no mail from her?

No one knew yet whether Wake was in danger. The news on the radio had dealt mostly with the devastation at Pearl, the fires and sunken ships, the dead sailors and terrified civilians, the blow to America's pride and the almost instantaneous lines forming at recruiting stations across the country. The end of peace.

Maggie had called the Morrison Knudsen offices this morning, but they couldn't say if their workers were safe. And she'd called the governor's office and the air base on the outskirts of Boise. No one could tell her anything. It was as if Wake Island didn't exist.

"Is it cold by the window? Do you want my sweater?" Agnes offered.

Maggie shook her head without looking up. Eddie reached over to pat her hands. She moved them into her lap.

The music stopped. And through the crackling airwaves President Roosevelt's voice filled the kitchen:

Yesterday, December 7, 1941—a date which will live in infamy—the United States of America was suddenly and deliberately attacked by naval and air forces of the Empire of Japan . . .

Maggie rose, clutching the kitchen counter with both hands. She stared at the radio on the counter, the President's voice pounding in her ears:

. . .Last night, Japanese forces attacked Hong Kong. Last night, Japanese forces attacked Guam. Last night, Japanese forces attacked the Philippine Islands. Last night, the Japanese attacked Wake Island . . .

She felt herself sliding to the floor, almost as if she were sliding into a bathtub, feeling weightless as if there really were water to buoy her. Eddie dropped down beside her, wrapped her tightly in his arms. Her mother crouched in front of her, clasping her hands. The tile floor was cool beneath her dress and her gaze fixed on a dark scuff rising from the base of the white kitchen cabinet like a column of black smoke swirling into a cloudy sky.

Though his mouth was near her ear, Eddie's voice sounded low and hollow, as if traveling through water. "Don't worry, honey. Everything's going to be all right."

She closed her eyes, feeling she deserved their pity and protectiveness. She wasn't strong, as she'd promised herself to be. She was numb—and Eddie's arms were warm and soothing. She accepted the glass of water her mother held out to her and sipped obediently.

She would let them care for her now because she needed them to, but when this numbness wore off and she stood against the force of her fear, she vowed to face it alone in her room, surrounded by photographs of Colin and by the things he had given her. She would teach herself to be strong for his sake. She would teach herself to believe he could yet come home.

Wake Island

Sharp coral fragments dug into Colin's knees. He'd been stripped to his undershorts and could feel the sun slowly burning his back and the soles of his feet. Before the Japanese had taken his clothing, he'd painfully removed the largest piece of shrapnel from his arm and tied a sock around the wound and the few tiny shrapnel pieces still embedded inside. A guard had confiscated the photograph of Chaplain's daughters and torn it in half, scattering the pieces at Colin's feet. He'd glared at Colin, challenging. Colin tried to look defiant, but his right eye began to twitch, and he was forced to look away. The guard grunted his disgust and bumped Colin hard as he passed.

A medic had bandaged Red's shoulder but left Colin's wound untreated as he rushed to help a seriously injured civilian. Though his elbow ached terribly, Colin's more urgent concern was the wire with which he had been bound. The Japanese had tied his hands behind his back—ignoring his cries of pain—then strung the wire around his neck. If he relaxed his shoulders or let his arms drop, the wire would strangle him. Though the guards had tied Red's hands, at least they hadn't run the wire to his neck. His wounded shoulder could never have supported the weight.

The prisoners had been instructed to keep silent, but when the guards occasionally circled to share cigarettes, Colin whispered to Red. "If they know we're civilians, maybe they'll treat us better."

"Don't count on it," Red said weakly. "Even though we aren't military, we still fought against them. That should only give them more reason to hate us."

"Do you think they'll shoot us?"

"Maybe. Unless they want to save ammunition. Then they could just march us into the sea with our hands tied and let us drown."

"I'm not going to die that way," Colin said. "I'll run first. *Make* them shoot me."

Somewhere the battle continued. Communications had been cut, and Major Devereux must still be working his way around the island ordering pockets of resistance to surrender. Colin nursed the vain hope that somehow the Japanese could still be defeated.

The guards finally waved their arms for the men to rise. Colin did so slowly, the joints in his knees popping loudly. The prisoners were arranged into two rows, and the guards kicked at their ankles to get them moving. Overhead, a Japanese plane exploded, shot down by the remaining free Americans, its parts raining over the island. The men jostled one another excitedly and grinned, until the guards cursed and kicked them harder.

They were marched to the airfield, where they were finally untied. Holding his elbow close to him, Colin rolled the tension from his shoulders and rubbed at painful indentations on his wrist. To his surprise, the men were directed toward a pile of confiscated clothing. Colin snatched a pair of shorts and one of the last shirts, which he draped over Red's shoulders. They sat down on the runway, and the guards aimed machine guns at their chests.

As the hours passed, Colin searched the faces of each new arrival for his friends. Frank came first, dragged from a hospital truck and dropped to the ground. He crawled to the front row and sat cross-legged, his head in his hands. Colin knew he'd been admitted to the hospital the night before with dysentery, but was still dismayed to see the boy looking so pale and shaken.

Patrick arrived shortly after Frank, winking nervously at Colin as the guards shoved him toward the back. His face was covered with dried blood, and his left calf was wrapped in a bloody bandage. When Marty arrived with a handful of Marines, Colin finally relaxed a little, though he couldn't stop feeling someone was missing, couldn't fully accept that Chaplain was not the man sitting to his left.

"I still can't figure out what's keeping our reinforcements," Colin whispered.

"They're not coming," said the man that should have been Chaplain. "Commander Cunningham got a message from Pearl during the battle. Our task force was recalled."

"You're lying."

"Like hell. I heard it straight from Cunningham's aide."

"Then that's it," Red whispered.

Colin hung his head and closed his eyes. In Boise, his mother would be hanging the Christmas wreath, his sister, Gwen, would be wrapping presents. Maggie would be baking sweet rolls for the neighbors, and Eddie would be shoveling the walk. Colin imagined himself among them, feeling the crisp winter air on his face.

A sharp kick brought him back to reality. A Japanese soldier was gesturing for him to straighten the line. Colin repositioned himself, his eyes on the soldier's back. His right eye twitched again, but this time with hatred, not fear. He promised himself that if he did not die today, he would fight with every ounce of strength left in him to survive this war. No matter what it took, he would see Maggie and his family again.

For the next fifty-four hours, the men were left in the open. The first cold night, Colin dug into the warm earth with his hands to escape the chilling wind and rain. Then during the day, the sun scorched his bare back and neck, and he could think of nothing but water.

On Christmas Day, the men were finally issued tainted water brought in gasoline barrels. A Japanese admiral strode across the airfield dressed in a stark white uniform, wearing ribbons and a sword. The men began to jeer until the guards fired a volley over their heads. An interpreter came forward to read a proclamation. Colin raised his head to listen, his eyes on the stony features of the man who'd been introduced as Admiral Kajioka, the man in whose hands rested the fate of the hundreds of men huddled together on the runway. In broken English, the interpreter began:

"Here it is proclaimed that the entire island of Wake are now the state-property of the Great Empire of Japan," the interpreter read. "— Japan who loves peace and respects justice has been obliged to take arms against the challenge of President Roosevelt. Therefore, in accordance with the peace-loving spirit of the Great Empire of Japan, Japanese Imperial Navy will not inflict any harms on those people—though they have been our enemy—who do not hold hostility against us in any respect. So, they be in peace!"

"Does that mean they're not going to kill us, Red?" Colin asked.

"At least not now."

The interpreter paused, staring into the faces of the Americans. His voice rose and became threatening. *"But whoever violates our spirit or whoever are not obedient shall be severely punished by our martial law."*

Kajioka turned, and Colin followed his gaze to the top of the flag mast where a battered American flag barely stirred in the trade winds. Colin realized what must happen next. He cursed under his breath as two soldiers stepped forward. With each squeak of the pulley, as the American flag was lowered, Colin folded in upon himself, feeling it as a blow to his stomach. Red leaned against him, shaking his head.

When Colin raised his eyes at last to see the banner of the Rising Sun snapping at the top of the flagpole, tears streaked his sunburned face. But he did not look away.

He vowed never to look away again.